...ikets

Would

Sing

Crickets Would Sing

Short fiction/Memoir by
Frances Fabri

Plum Branch Press
Harrisburg, PA

For information about permission to reproduce selections
from this book, write to Permissions, Plum Branch Press,
P.O. Box 5104, Harrisburg, PA 17110-0104

LCCN: 2006928806
ISBN: 9780970272034

Cover design by Marjaneh Talebi
Cover print, "The Flowering Mind," by David Moyer
Interior design by Michele Waters
Editorial assistance by Diane Thompson

Printed in the United States of America

10 9 8 7 6 5 4 3 2

For Sylvie and Matt

Table of Contents

Any
Ordinary
Day

It is over now, she thinks; any chance we had to save him is gone, gone with the night. When Mrs. Morvay looks out the window at five o'clock in the morning, the sky is cloudless. It would be a bright day. She glances once more at the sky and then carries herself wearily into the kitchen.

The kitchen is cool with something of the twilight still caught in it. She halts in its center not knowing what to do. Then she walks to the table and sits on the stool.

She sits hunched and heavy, thinking again of the passed night and then of the passed days—irrevocably gone—and of what her son Sandor said, "Act like this day is any ordinary day, do your chores, mind your own business." And she thinks Sandor will be doing just that—minding his own business, just like the rest of the village.

By now he is standing in the golden fields at his farm far from the village, just like the rest. The wheat is undulating in the morning breeze like a gentle, golden sea, and he stands, as always before reaping, looking far away, his eyes gleaming in the shadow of his straw hat. Then he starts, moving slowly, rhythmically in the sunshine, and the wheat lies in glistening rows in his wake and the sun bounces from the blade of his scythe at each sweep.

"Act like it is any ordinary day, just like everyone else," he said last night before he and his wife Eszter left for the farm. They had come to the village, as they always do before the harvest, and stayed with her. She and Sandor argued throughout the three-day visit. Last night was merely the end.

"Now look, Mother, we can't hide him," Sandor said. "You have to understand. I hate this too." They sat around the table. Eszter was crying, her face red and shiny in the lamplight.

"We'll never get another doctor as good as he is," Estzer said, as though only that matters—how good a doctor they would have.

"He was a fine man," Sandor said. *"Was,"* he said, as though Doctor Mandel were already.... Oh, God. She couldn't hold any more. Strange words rained like a torrent, words she had never used before, while Sandor and Eszter sat silent and red faced.

It was the way the two of them sat there, she remembers clearly now, that brought her mind back. She was as surprised at her own outburst as they were. Then Sandor bellowed, pounding the table...in his mother's house, too!

"It's not *us*! It's not *us* who are doing this!" he screamed, his eyes bloodshot, his head thrust forward and lowered. She looked into his bloodshot eyes, throughout the bellowing and throughout the silence that followed. "Why me? Hasn't he got other patients? I have Eszter and the family to think about, and you too Mother. You want to get us killed, is that it? You've seen the German posters. You've read their papers.

Now look, it *is* just an internment. It *really* is. The doctor will be back after the war."

Then like a wounded beast, he yelled, "Quit looking at me!"

And, tearing his eyes from hers he added, "And quit your preaching."

As though she hadn't already quit.

Later, he said other things, more calmly, about war and foreign occupation and politics and about how sorry he felt for Doctor Mandel. "Such a fine man," he said, and how he felt sorry for the rest too, but nothing could be done.

Other people also felt bad. "And," he added, "neither Doctor Mandel nor the others expected any help because they knew nothing could be done." Then he talked again about how one could only think of his family in times like these.

She felt old suddenly and very tired. She hoped they would go. She would go to bed and sleep.

But she didn't. When they finally left, she just sat at the table, looking into the lamp's light, thinking of her son standing at the door before leaving, saying quietly and bitterly, "You just don't *want* to understand."

Later she stood and walked to the chest. The Bible lay there, black and gold on the white doily. She took it to the table, sat down slowly, heavily. She opened it at random.

"If the foundations be destroyed, what can the righteous do?" cried out the psalm-singing Jewish king. Her hand trembled as she turned the page. But no matter how many times she read what followed, there was no answer.

But wasn't the answer clear anyway? Not stated, maybe, because there was no need to state it: *Each* has to find her own way.

"But I'm old, my Lord," she cried into the quiet room, addressing Him as she had learned to do these past three weeks. "I'm a simple woman. How can *I* know? How can *I* find the way?"

Much later, she thinks she knows a way, poor as it is. She falls asleep relieved.

Looking back from the calm morning, she realizes that way doesn't make sense. She would go to Doctor Mandel's house. She has to go, but she doesn't know why, and she doesn't know what she would do there. After weeks of worrying, she is so weary, it doesn't matter.

It is different now. Since she has given her farm to Sandor, she has no place she can hide a man. That's clear. Clear, too, is that going to Doctor Mandel's house makes no sense.

She can only heed her son: "You can't do a thing; you just have to accept it."

Accept it. Do her daily chores. "Try not to think about it," Sandor said. She looks around the kitchen. She feels its cool quiet surround her. She smells its bread, fruit, fresh linen. She should move around in its midst, the way she always has done, and will until the end. Nothing can be done—the posters and the papers, the gendarmes and the Germans. And as everybody says, it's just an internment, nothing worse. Besides it is not *her* business; it is not *she* to whom it is done, and it is not *she* who is doing it. It is not *her* sin. Her life is in this kitchen. There are others, younger than she, for whom Doctor Mandel has done more. So why should she—

She weeps then, loud, unabashedly.

Finally, it's over. She hunches over the table, thinking that never in her life has she been this weary, this drained. She feels weighted and yet empty.

Suddenly, she thinks of Doctor Mandel. It is strange. Hasn't she been thinking of him all along? Yet somehow he has vanished in the storm of who is doing it, who is not; who should do what, and why; and "What should the righteous do?" Somewhere he has gotten lost, Doctor Mandel. Doctor Mandel, who waits alone in that old house of his, to be taken....

She wipes her hot, tear-softened face, then stands and walks to the window. The sky is so blue this morning it hurts her eyes.

I *shall* go to Doctor Mandel, she thinks.

She washes and dresses fast, yet with care, putting on her heavy, black damask dress, her Sunday best, and enters the quiet, early-morning street. It isn't until she reaches the corner that she notices her Bible. She can't recall taking it off the chest. It must be on account of putting on her Sunday dress, she finally decides. Anyhow, the Bible is clasped in her left hand, reminding her of the church's whiteness on summer Sundays, of the smell of starched clothes, and of King David's psalms rising between the white walls. It feels good to hold it.

The streets are quiet; she hasn't met a soul. True, it is harvest time and all are at their farms. Still...and then she remembers what her son had said about his not doing it to Doctor Mandel. Neither do these others, she thinks, passing the silent, solid, whitewashed houses.

Her big shadow moves slowly in front of her on the empty, sunlit street.

———

Doctor Mandel watches the sun emerge from the dark night, the walls first gray, then pallid-white. The instruments glitter silver and the walls dazzle white when hit by the first rays.

It is morning now, the sky blue as cornflowers. He pushes his chair from the desk and stands. He has to wash, shave, pack. Time is running out. Yet he keeps looking at his office, thinking he likes it best as it looks now, at this hour, and on such a sunny day— bright and ready for patients, as it has been for thirty-seven years.

Never again. It is over, even if it turns out to be just an internment. He knows this with certainty, although he doesn't know how or why. He feels stronger than ever it descend on him like a low, dense, wintry cloud. Then he feels that sensation of a hand gripping his heart, holding it fast, as it has in the last few weeks.

He sighs, walks around the office, halting here and there, touching this and that, seeing it all clear and sharp. Then he looks out the window.

The street is empty. A man passes by. Through the white gauze curtains he sees the man as though through a mist. Maybe that is how those about to die saw him as he sat at their bedsides.

On Post Street Mrs. Morvay sees someone—a little boy in a garden behind a low, white picket fence. He stands with his back to her, leaning against the fence. At her steps he turns around. The yellow star stands out sharp against his blue shirt.

Although only seven o'clock, it's hot. Gendarme Sergeant Zador marches with Corporal Gaspar along the quiet, empty streets, feels the sweat trickle down his forehead and his neck. This uniform with its black hat and black cock feathers looks sharp but is damned hot, and this dustbin village is an oven.

Of course, it's better than the Russian Front, even with all its briefings, instructions and other nonsense. Soon it will be over. The Jews will be rounded up, herded into the old brick factory and transported by train to who knows where.

If the Germans want the Jews, they should get them. Why should he have to do their dirty work, but orders are orders. What if the Germans lose the war? He'll be mixed up in this dirty business. But they won't lose. There are just some setbacks.

Corporal Gaspar is sweating too. Good, and he was born here. He should be used to this heat.

Then Sergeant Zador remembers the warrants. Damn it, life is not fair. All three families live so far apart. Klein, Lieb and Mandel—*Doctor* Mandel. What nerve.

In front of the cinema is one of those warning posters. Good, although he doesn't have to worry about these stupid peasants doing anything. They are such dumb cowards. Sergeant Zador smirks under his mustache. If he were in Budapest drinking with his buddies, he would bet on it.

He'll get the Doctor first. He turns left. Colonel Gaspar follows like the good peasant he is.

Why the devil do the Germans want these Jews anyway? Someone at the station told him the Germans are having a labor shortage.

But then that Liptak, he's a card. He said the Germans will just march them to the wall. "Bang, bang," he said, raising his arms as though aiming, "Bang, bang, and no more Jewish question."

―――――――――――――――

Three families, Mrs. Morvay realizes sadly. The street is still quiet, the whitewashed houses silent. She presses the Bible against her breast. For a fleeting second she hears the psalms of David, soaring on hundreds of voices on Sunday mornings. But then, she thinks, could we ever, after this day, my Lord, sing praise again?

―――――――――――――――

He should be thinking of the others, Doctor Mandel tells himself, and of packing his satchel conscientiously with medicines, instruments. He should stop daydreaming.

What first, he wonders, then removes from the cabinet a small steel case. Hypodermic syringes, their needles sharp and steely, lay in the case, glittering in their tiny racks. Clean. Sure. Tempting.

He snaps the case shut. His fingers tighten firmly over it. No, he thinks. He has gone over that often enough. He can't because of the others. Anyhow, has not death always lurked close to him? Now it's just closer.

He could still work; he might still help. His work gives him meaning. Warm memories loosen the grip around his heart for only a second, for also come memories of bed-sides where he could only witness in vain. He, the doctor, would vanish, and only he, the man, would sit, his heart beating steadily, his lean body functioning as usual as he would witness another man's dying.

He remembers eyes, dimming, looking into his. All he could do was look back into those eyes, feel that futile urge to reach across the fast opening gap. "Here I am," he would try to say with his eyes, the foolish man he would be. "You are not alone."

Alone? Suddenly he feels the word echo inside him. The room grows cavernous with that word now bouncing off the icy walls. This room is empty in a world seething with people he has ministered to in joy and in agony. He thinks he will scream in pain, scream into the silent vault the room has become.

Then he recovers. After all, the question of his getting any help, just like the question of using the needles, has been settled.

He puts the case into the satchel.

Sergeant Zador and Corporal Gaspar's boots hit the sidewalk sharply at the same times. Their bayonets, when they cross Post Street, reflect impressively from a shop window.

"Quite some house the Jew has," Zador says when he sees it down the block, the long buff brick house with a big, brown door. What big shot is going to grab it after he has done all the work? There's no justice.

The door creaks when he throws it open and then a bell rings. He almost trips on the high threshold. Caspar starts to grin. Zador must preserve his authority. The door slams behind them, and the long hall is dark, like a grave. And the bell keeps ringing, cling, cling, cling. That Jew has rigged up something fancy. Zador wants to find that bell, smash it against.... Nonsense, he tells himself and spits.

The little bell will tinkle when she opens the door, thinks Mrs. Morvay, a block from Doctor Mandel's house; and the hall will be cool. The smell of medicine, disinfectant, whatever doctors use—will meet her in the hall as it always has. Then there will be the office, and Doctor Mandel— Oh, Lord, what can she say....

She fears she will turn and flee, back along the deserted streets, but then she clenches the Bible and draws a deep breath.

This uppity Jew should look like a Jew thinks Zador. He shouldn't stand tall, erect behind his desk, staring, his hands calm on that stupid satchel doctors run around with. Everything about this Jew is wrong, nervy bastard. He needs to be taught a lesson.

Never mind, he will follow orders and make it as smooth as possible. Let the Germans teach this Jew some manners.

"Doctor Mandel," he says. It doesn't sound right, so he clears his throat and starts again, "Doctor...."

The front door creaks, that stupid bell tinkles, then stops, and then slow, heavy steps clop down the hall. Who the devil? Then he sees an old, peasant woman appear at the office door.

She is thickset and dressed in black, carrying a Bible of all things, in her rough, stumpy hand, as though she were going to church. Sergeant Zador can't help but hold back a relieved grin.

"Well, you are hedging your bets aren't you, old woman, carrying your Bible to the Doctor's office. If the Doctor can't cure you, then God Almighty will. But, the office is closed today." He notices a glint of admiration on Gaspar's face—not so dumb for a country lad.

But she doesn't hear him, doesn't even look. She walks straight to the Jew, slow and steady. When she reaches the desk she stops.

"No office hours. Don't you hear me?" Zador says.

The woman just looks into the Jew's eyes.

The Jew says quietly, "I can't attend to you, Mrs. Morvay."

"Now get out, you old raven!" says Sergeant Zador.

She stands with her back to Sergeant Zador, big and black and silent.

Sergeant Zador steps to the desk. After all, just how long would he, with his authority—but then he stops, for there is something strange about the way they stand, the two, facing each other, staring at each other. He should stop this nonsense, but his orders are to make it smooth, so he will wait.

The Doctor and the old peasant woman don't speak.

"Thank you, Mrs. Morvay," says the Doctor. "Thank you." Now why the devil is he thanking her? They both are insane. Then the doctor says, real quiet, "Good-bye now, Mrs. Morvay."

But she just stands there, the stubborn peasant that she is, looking at the Doctor.

And then the Doctor—can you believe it—begins to smile, kind of strangely, but he does, and he reaches across the desk and presses her big peasant hands. That old raven smiles back.

"Doctor Mandel," Sergeant Zador says, for it sure is more than enough time.

"I'm ready," says Doctor Mandel.

Your
Task

"I want three lists tomorrow morning. Eight o'clock sharp."

The Sturmbannfuehrer sits in the former Council Elder's chair tapping on the top of his white desk with a small red cigarette lighter.

Liebner stands across the desk on the white Persian rug which used to be in Dr. Silberman's stolen living room but is now in his surgery stretching from the desk to where the examining table once was.

"The first should list every member in the Ghetto between fifteen and fifty-five."

"Herr Sturmbannfuehrer, all records were lost when the synagogue was destroyed," says Liebner, his fist tightening over his crumpled *barret*, his felt prayer hat.

"Council Elder, I am not interested how you get your task done."

The Sturmbannfuehrer reaches into his pocket, draws out a silver cigarette case and extricates a long, foreign-looking cigarette.

"The second list should contain all children under fifteen."

He snaps the cigarette case closed. It sounds like a gunshot on a wintry morning.

"The third list...." He halts now, cigarette between pursed lips, and triggers the lighter. Liebner watches the tiny light flare then disappear as the cap springs down upon it.

"On the third list I want the names of all over fifty-five."

"Herr Sturmban...."

"And no tricks, Liebner. Remember what happened at the farmyard."

Outside, level with Liebner's eyes, the bright sun is suspended from the early morning sky. Blinded momentarily, Liebner stumbles.

"To the left," orders the guard walking him back to the Ghetto where they keep them until...until what?

Liebner walks the wide empty street flanked by barren trees reaching with stark branches toward the sky. A man emerges from a house down the street. Abstracted, rummaging in his briefcase, he walks toward Liebner and the guard. When he looks up, he quickly crosses to the other side of the street.

Around the corner looms the courthouse, its peaked roof piercing the sky. On a day like this, clerks in drafty rooms would be blowing on their fingers thinks Liebner. And in an ornate high-ceilinged room an old man with frosty hair would peer from his high oaken bench upon someone standing there, tight in his Sunday-best, waiting for the verdict.

Outside the courthouse entrance stands a woman bundled in a fox coat, talking to a bespectacled man wearing a fur hat with its flaps turned up. As Liebner and the guard approach, the woman stops talking. Then with wide blue eyes lit up, she speaks quietly to the man. The man laughs in hard, sharp bursts that follow Liebner to the next corner.

Around the corner he sees his home, stolen last year by the Germans, narrow between two wider houses. On the ground floor the bakery door is open, and the aroma of fresh bread wafts into the street, and is surely wafting up his narrow staircase, and into his office facing the street, and into his small apartment behind the office.

Liebner looks up at the windows of his stolen office. The drapes are drawn, the same maroon drapes. They kept the drapes. Did they keep the rest, the desk with the leather top, the massive bookcases?

Do they feel comfortable in the home he returned to— stealing along the deserted streets on that sultry night so he could scrub the crusted blood from his body and shave the scraggly beard he had grown fighting in the forest?

Across the street in front of old Levy's grocery a husky man stands in a blue denim apron. He spits in a high arc, the spittle landing halfway across the street. He turns and enters old Levy's stolen shop, the bell clinking, as always, as the man opens and then closes the door.

Liebner wonders whether the shop is as messy as it used to be, and as warm. Old Levy's granddaughter, a skinny redhead, after school used to dash about arranging bins on the shelves and filling glass jars with colored candy on the counter.

Then, one day.... It was a cold day just like this one. No, it wasn't like this one, how could it have been? Anyway, on a cold day, the redhead flew from the shop. A long green scarf, like windblown grass rippled behind her. Her hair, flaming in the sunshine and dancing around her face, flicked into Liebner when the girl collided with him as he passed with measured steps in his buttoned brown coat with the beaver collar and his brown fedora.

"Sorry," said the girl laughing. Her breath was warm and smelled of cinnamon. She tossed back her head, sending her red hair cascading over the green scarf.

Then she flew away.

That flaming, curly mess—copper? Hard to say. Also, hard to say whether she was pretty or not. Her little face was like a triangle propped on its narrowest point. No, not pretty really. And yet.... And how old was she, could she have been, on that sparkling day? Sixteen? No, not a child anymore, Levy's granddaughter.

How old had he been, thirty-three? Was it two years ago? If the collision had happened at all; if a life had existed in which such small episodes happened.

———————

How fast they reach the barbed wire and wood Ghetto gate. Two guards pull the gate open, let him in, then shut it behind him with the help of his guard. The three guards stomp and rub their hands outside the gate, as Liebner stands alone in the Ghetto street. He jams his hands into his pockets and walks to the corner, turns into a narrow street out of the guards' sight.

The street is as shadowy as it was the day his group was marched into it and ordered to stand near that stone bench set into the house wall. Three old women sat down right away, their arms around those lumpy bundles in their laps. He remembers them being chased away and disappearing into the crowds while their bundles were tossed by laughing guards until they fell apart, their contents scattered: a fringed babushka landing on the bench, a prayer book broken into pieces on the cobbles, sepia photos fluttering around like autumn leaves. That day, he stood in the crowd, his brown coat loose over his gaunt body, sinewy since the forest—not lawyer Liebner's flabby body, but a ghost fighter's lean body from the forest.

Now Liebner pounds his steps on the cobbles. He flails up one street, down another, lost. Are the houses really swaying...their steep roofs touching across the street?

He leans against a wall with his heart pounding, removes his *barret* and presses his forehead against the cold crumbling stones.

Under fifteen; over fifty-five.

Liebner stands at the window, scratching off flakes of peeling brown paint from the sill. Behind him, the small stuffy room; in front of him, the street, and beyond the street, other streets with houses and rooms reeking of bodies...ten to a room? Rooms he lived in before he was forced to accept the Council Elder title.

Under fifteen, over fifty-five? Many.

Over fifteen and under fifty-five? Few left. Women mostly. The men were conscripted for labor, except Nathan Hoffer who is blind, and Ben Salzman who is lame and a few like him who were overlooked or forgotten. What matters is not this, but what that fiend said was "your task."

There is a knock on the door. Old Levy shuffles in without waiting. He wears Liebner's brown coat. The shabby coat reaches to his shoes. The beaver collar is gone—swapped, maybe for a bowl of soup or a chunk of bread. Still, as always, old Levy comments, "Fine fabric. Nothing like English woolens. Lasts forever. Warm, but light!"

He runs his palms along the coat from neck to waist.

"What's going on?"

Old Levy is keeping a journal, recording whatever happens. "For all to know when this is over." Now, how does he imagine—well, it was his granddaughter who talked him into it when it all began. Anyway, besides keeping the old man busy, it has turned him into a nuisance.

He pulls a copybook from the pocket of his coat and a stubby pencil. He licks the tip of the pencil, then poises it over the copybook.

"What's new? What needs to be recorded?"

"Nothing!" Liebner hears himself scream. "You understand, old man? Nothing!"

Wide now, the pale, gray eyes peer at him through wire-rimmed spectacles.

"Why do you haunt me?" Liebner yells. "Why?"

Old Levy straightens to his full height, whatever that is—five-feet?

"Becoming Council Elder has gone to your head," he says leaving.

Shaking, Liebner walks to the window. In the street he sees the old man bent as he shuffles away, the "fine English woolens" flapping against the filthy sidewalk in front of him.

Liebner turns from the window. Near the desk, on the worn planks of the floor lies the precious stubby pencil. He picks it up.

Liebner rolls it between his palms. The pencil becomes moist all over. From his own sweat? He dashes from the room, down the steps, along the street.

At the corner he searches. The old man is gone.

He walks back slowly, then looks up at his window. No maroon drapes here, just a drooping blackout shade for his office...his cell?

Well, he likes being alone, not squeezed against others, not listening on sleepless nights to snoring, to crying and to the Hoffers making love in the dark, the Hoffers, never minding the remarks, funny, caustic, obscene or envious.

Yes, it's nice to be alone.

"Offices of the Council," says a cardboard sign on his front door. "Offices" according to the Germans: one tiny room across the landing with two pews facing each other salvaged from the synagogue. The pews smell like exhumed coffins. The room is no more than three paces wide.

Liebner climbs the creaking steps and enters the "Offices." Just inside the door, Rachel Berg sits at a table covered with papers, wrapped in the huge, fluffy black thing she calls an afghan, with her gray hair like a thatched roof over her pale face.

Rachel Berg, well over fifty-five.

Over her glasses she looks at Liebner. "Feldman was here to complain about...."

"Send for the Council to see me at two P.M.," says Liebner.

"All right," says Rachel. "Now, Feldman complained...."

"To hell with Feldman," screams Liebner. "Just send for the damned Council."

"All right, but...."

"Shut up," screams Liebner. "Just shut up and do as you are told."

"Now listen, Liebner...."

Liebner turns away from her and steps to a pew where Schneider sits in Council meetings, Schneider who is in his eighties; and next to him sits Kaufman, at least seventy; and Chaim Kupfer who is sixty. Over fifty-five, all the Council members.

Liebner strikes the pew hard with his palm and winces as a splinter drives into his flesh.

"Serves you right," says Rachel Berg.

"Don't send for the bloody Council," shrieks Liebner. "You hear me?" And he slams his aching palm down on Rachel Berg's table, sending papers flying.

—————

All right, no Council meeting but then what?

Oh, to hell with it! How did he ever get into this, he, Josef Liebner! Lawyer! Bachelor! Minding his own business all his life. He was even pushed into the resistance. Just what good did it do, what good did they achieve fighting in the forest until it ended with friends' bodies falling on him, hiding his quivering body?

—————

Before the farmyard, the Council had refused to talk to the Germans. Early that morning, the nine Council members were marched from town. Flanked by the Sturmbannfuehrer's men, up and down hills they hiked on a country road. Shivering, Liebner kept his eyes on the ground wondering where that road would take them. Then for some reason they stopped, and Dr. Silberman said, "My God! Just look at that, Liebner." Liebner saw Dr. Silberman's arm sweep across the countryside. It was as though the curtain that had always hung between him and everything else was drawn wide open.

They looked down on a valley, wide and shimmering with silvery frost. Scattered were clumps of barren trees. Roads like narrow ribbons seemed thrown between houses. Smoke rose from chimneys into the ice-colored sky. Dotting the valley were houses, surely with huge country kitchens with roaring fireplaces and tables with people sitting around them—a man, a woman, kids too, and maybe some old people—right now as they would every morning of their lives.

Liebner wished he could hike down into that valley, knock on the door of one of those houses and join a family in their warm kitchen, sit next to them at their table, feel their warm bodies next to his body.

"Move," yelled Sturmbannfuehrer's men.

So on they marched, up and down hills again, except now the world was clear to Liebner. The barren trees along the road with their branches reached this way and that, no two trees alike, nor even two twigs, each glorious in its own way, not to speak of the sky, gradually turning from icy-gray to light powdery blue. How marvelous was the way Dr. Silberman's breath danced in the cold air around his head with its silky white mane.

If only this march would go on forever, thought Liebner.

But then, at the end of another dirt road was the farmhouse or what was left of it. Tufts of dry weeds spilled from gaping holes where windows had been. The Council members stood looking at the farmhouse and at each other. A shiny black car made its way up the hill and stopped. Out emerged Sturmbannfuehrer, lithe in his immaculate uniform.

They were marched around the house. The farmyard was huge, stretching from the house to a weatherbeaten barn. And barren, too, that yard. All over were foot prints preserved in frozen mud—and bodies. Round and round the Sturmbannfuehrer ordered them to walk, round and round bodies scattered in the yard. They lay as they must have fallen. Face up, face sideways, face down;

legs together, legs apart, arms underneath, arms pressing the ground.

The young woman had one arm under her body, the other stretched on the ground with her small hand dipped half-way into the frozen mud, her pointed face lying sideways on a cushion of copper hair caked with mud.

Liebner stopped and stared, shaking.

"Move," yelled the Sturmbannfuehrer.

And on and on they stumbled around the bodies.

"Halt," yelled the Sturmbannfuehrer.

Liebner tore his eyes from her body and looked at the Sturmbannfuehrer holding in his gloved hand a small crop made of shiny brown leather.

"These people had guns," he said. "Five of them. Why, they even had some ammunition. And guess where we learned about the guns?" he smiled as he looked at them for a second. Then with his elegant crop he waved across the valley below the farmyard, white in its wintry beauty with its pretty houses.

Then the Council members were marched to the barn and lined along it with their backs to the wall.

"The Council Elder is to stand in the center," the Sturbannfuehrer ordered. Dr. Silberman moved to the center next to Liebner. Facing them, across the trampled ground, the Sturmbannfuehrer's men raised their guns. Deep, endless silence soaked the air. A raven flew above them and cawed. Liebner listened to Dr. Silberman's slow, raspy breath. Then Liebner forgot about him as he felt the air, cold and moist, settle on his face like an icy mask. He closed his eyes. His body stiffened, and he wasn't breathing.

Maybe I am dead already, he thought. Didn't even notice it happen. How nice.

"Fire," ordered the Sturmbannfuehrer.

The guns ripped the silence of the farmyard.

Liebner opened his eyes and saw Dr. Silberman crumple to the ground.

But the rest of the Council still stood there—he also, not happily gone, facing the men with the guns.

Finally, the Sturmbannfuehrer spoke. "You people like to talk. Well now, back to the Ghetto. And talk."

And they would talk, of course, eventually. The lesson taught in the farmyard would be driven home as intended. That evening, however, back in the "Offices of the Council," they sat silently facing each other in the coffin-smelling pews.

Finally, Chaim Kupfer said, "Somebody will have to talk to the Germans, to be Council Elder...Liebner, will you?"

"Now, Liebner, it's not as though you don't deserve it, but let me take that splinter out of your palm."

Liebner holds his hand over the washbasin and lets Rachel Berg deftly coax the splinter out with a needle held between her spotted fingers.

No nonsense, Rachel is. Never married. An accountant.

"Thank you," says Liebner. "Listen, Rachel, what would you do if you had to...?"

"If what?"

"If—well, never mind. It's nothing, Rachel, nothing."

He opens the door for her, watches her step reluctantly to the landing. She turns back.

"Liebner, if there's anything...."

"There isn't," says Liebner closing the door. Then he leans against it, eyeing the room—the cot, the battered desk, the old-fashioned wash basin with its chipped bowl.

Lawyer Liebner's "Offices."

"You as a lawyer...." someone said that day in the room with coffin-smelling pews.

Dr. Silberman's crumpled body....

"As a lawyer, you might be able to reason...." said another.

That body with the mud-caked copper hair that one winter morning had danced around a radiant little face....

Had they really thought he would agree to take Dr. Silberman's place after that morning? But the Council sat, waiting.

———

Chaim Kupfer sits on the cot in Liebner's "Offices," his once-white pharmacist's coat hanging from under a huge, greasy brown jacket. Liebner paces from door to window, his arms flailing.

"Chaim," he says, "you heard this story from your brother, and he heard it from the man he used to play bridge with, and he in turn...."

"All right, Liebner. You think it's a rumor, or a lie, or who knows what you think.... Anyway, you don't believe it."

"Come on, Chaim, this is crazy. Who has ever heard of...why, I don't even know what to call it—Selective Pogrom? Production-line Pogrom?"

Chaim sits still as Liebner flails.

"And the source is a school teacher who plays half-wit cleaning woman and goes through files at headquarters. That's nuts."

He stops by Chaim and clasps his hands behind the small of his back.

"Do you expect me to believe this script for a bizarre movie?" Liebner says, glaring for a silent moment at Chaim. Then he paces again, his hands still clasped behind his back. "And as to the evidence...."

"Quit playing courtroom, Liebner," says Chaim, his voice shrill now, as though not his voice at all. Then, after a while, Chaim says softly, "Come sit, Liebner," as he pats the cot.

Liebner sits.

"Look, son, I don't want to believe it either."

Liebner springs up. "I don't want to believe it?"

"Yes, you don't want to believe it."

"Get out, Chaim. Just get out."

But Chaim doesn't, and he doesn't take offence either. He just stands and puts his dry hands over Liebner's and holds them tight.

"Listen, son. Whatever the situation is—I mean, right now—I could stay with you. Not as though you—I—or anyone could do anything. I could just stay with you, if you want."

Liebner yanks his hands from Chaim's. "Leave me alone."

Chaim walks to the door slowly and looks back at Liebner.

"Leave me alone," Liebner screams.

"Under fifteen; over fifty-five," said the Sturmbannfuehrer.

"Children and old people," had read the schoolteacher playing half-wit cleaning woman in Chaim's story.

Liebner stands at the window looking at the street. The dark envelops the stony, icy houses. In that house he had shared a room with Chaim, with whom he played chess in the yard and who beat him each and every time. Chaim, sixty. Liebner had shared the same house with little Golda, age four, maybe five, who would sit on the steps and sing something she had made up, in a shrill voice that got on people's nerves—shared also with Golda's mother and with Rachel, and others, too, and of course, with the Hoffers who would make love at night. And they were right, thinks Liebner. And he laughs. Proper, stuffy lawyer Liebner believes making love in a shared room—even if not dark—is right.

He stops laughing and looks at the sky. Stars are twinkling as stars have always done, would always do. He stands for two or three hours. Finally, he turns from the stars and the black felt canopy beyond them and gropes his way to the desk.

Elbows on desk, chin cupped in hand, he sits glaring into the dark room then pulls out a drawer and feels around until he finds the small copybook among the mess of papers.

He holds it in both hands as though it were as heavy as the old leather-bound record book, the one consumed in the roaring fire of the synagogue.

How had Rachel compiled this list of names, approximate dates of births, marriages, deaths?

"Just what good did fighting do?" Liebner had once asked himself while scrubbing off the forest grime, shaving his scraggly beard. A logical question, no doubt.

But then that question vanishes as Liebner sitting at the coffin-smelling desk tears pages from the copybook and shreds them into tiny bits.

Words

behind

the

Words

Once there was writing. And once there were students, their faces coming back now as Paul Langman sits on his suitcase, wedged between Mr. Schwartz and ancient Miss Agata Holzner. His back leans against the boxcar wall. His legs, numb by now, are somewhere between suitcases and bundles. Was it long ago? Yes, faces are coming back, faces in classrooms. Or not so long ago? Who knows as time becomes illusory in the eternal dimness of the boxcar, with day from night hardly discernible, with moments extending into eternity, but days slipping away fast, and the distant past being light years away, yet very clear; and the recent past a blurred bedlam.

Recent past? Why, even the present is blurred. Although that shouldn't be, now should it? He should be alert, should savor it, should drink it to the lees, this bitter, terrible cup.

But he is old, and he is tired. Would he ever, could he ever teach history or write again? Could anything he sees or experiences now benefit anyone? Why should he sharpen his mercifully dulled senses and mind?

Sharp, clear perception—his strange companion— friend sometimes, foe sometimes, has been forever there, part of him.

Around him there still is life. People huddle, breathing heavily, pressed tightly against each other, encased in the boxcar pulled by a sputtering engine through the alien night.

Toward what?

Toward death, Paul Langman thinks, toward death. He can't stop the thought as it races through his mind, his body, in rhythm with the wheels thundering under the boxcar floor.

Toward death: toward a blood-spattered wall, or toward a ditch in a faraway forest, or toward a chamber. No. It can't be. This is the wartime hysteria of people imagining things, of rumors growing into sick fantasizing.

It can't be. Aren't the known facts bad enough? But then what—what lies at the end of this journey?

A concentration camp?

A nightmarish concept. Not connected with anything experienced, a camp invokes in him vague, distant images: shadowy masses against eternal twilight—diffused, abstract, yet terribly permeating images of featureless suffering.

God! Just what would a concentration camp be like?

No one has ever been there. Rather, no one has ever returned to tell.

Outrages there, the rumors say, but to hell with the rumors. On the other hand, the rumors were right about the boxcars.

What is really happening is internment of undesirable elements...combined with an excellent chance to rob them of all they own.

A concentration camp? They can't—the Germans.... After all, they, too, are human beings.

Besides, they have already lost the war. Stalingrad. Italy. The Atlantic Wall. It is July 1944. Even they should know...should be anxious not to add to their...? Why, yes, there would be excesses, but as to those rumors, they are nonsense, of course.

But, death-*death*; death-*death*; death-*death*, rattle the wheels under the floor.

Paul Langman listens to that rattle, and to the beating of his heart, and then falls asleep.

When he wakes, a dim, gray light spreads inside the boxcar. Outside, in the world, it would be dawn. Automatically, he looks at his wrist. No watch there. Oh, yes, of course, no watch. That taken too. Well, it must be dawn, but what do hours or moments matter.

He is wide awake now, as he always is, right upon awakening. He feels keenly Mr. Schwartz' shriveled old body against him, also the bony elbow of Miss Holzner. And he smells the stink of humanity, unwashed and packed tightly for three days, and the stench of the latrine bucket, although, fortunately, it is at the other end of the boxcar.

He rubs his head. He tries softly to push Mr. Schwartz away and flexes his muscles as best he can.

The light becomes stronger. Outside it would be bright daylight. But inside it is as light as it will get with only four small windows way up under the roof. Still, it is light enough for him to see them—men, children, women—contorted forms crouching in the boxcar, its rough planks barely containing them.

Communal coffin, comes to him then, and he can't erase the thought. A light, dry, choking feeling, never before experienced, leaves him shivering when the thought finally passes.

But it passes only when people wake and the boxcar becomes alive with motion, with sound. Mr. Schwartz wakes and Miss Holzner smoothes out her dress, takes cookies from one of her many little satchels, arranges them on her palm and offers them to him as though offering them on a platter in her lacy little home. He accepts one with due formality and watches Miss Holzner eat the others, slowly, daintily, and sitting bolt upright.

It helps, Miss Holzner's little rite.

He stands, stretches his legs. Then, as so many times before, he steps onto his suitcase, grabs the bars of the window and looks out.

A station slides by. He doesn't catch the sign. The land is flat, the grass thin and bleached by the sun. Then the grass disappears, the ground becomes ash-gray. The train veers, and from one instant to the other, it all looms up.

It lies gray and stark in the morning sun that slants across it, slicing it into long strips of shadows. Stark shafts of light between the rows of barracks stretch to the horizon. Watchtowers dot the landscape like exclamation points. An eerie sparkling lights it all: the barbed wire fences twinkle in the sun.

So that's it, thinks Paul Langman, his throat dry, very dry.

He looks around. The train stretches away along the ramp, with the doors of the car open and people standing on the ramp dazed, or dashing and hollering, trying to find something or someone. The SS men bark commands and men in black and white striped convict clothes dash back and forth among the crowd. A group of officers down the ramp chat, greatly at ease it seems in the morning sunshine.

Paul Langman watches it all unfold. Because, even if it does seem sheer chaos, there is a method in it all. The convicts are separating the men and the women, that is evident, and they do so quickly. Up the ramp are herded the women, and down below, the men. And it goes fast, with much cursing and brutality from the convicts, but brutality not beyond a point, yet close to—what point? He doesn't know, just feels a suggestion of something in the air, something that would happen if those hands holding onto each other did not let go. Something emanates from the convicts. He seeks to know what it is. But at the same time, from the convicts comes reassurance. "You're going to the bath," they keep shouting. "To the bath. You can't go together. You'll meet in the barracks. After the bath."

"To the bath. To the bath," they yell, until finally it seems to float around them in the air, the word, "bath." Like magic, it feels, as though its refreshing effect has already come, sweeping away worries, doubts. Sensibly, even humanely, after that trip, a bath.

And after that, the barracks, as the convicts say over and over.

Yes, those barracks, all those barracks, for whom are they built if...?

And of course, there would be separate baths for men and women.

The women mill around on the ramp. They, too, talk about the bath. Shabby, haggard, their frightened eyes dart, all of them looking oddly alike.

Except one. In midst of the turmoil, she stands straight and hard. Her face is ageless, as though carved of sandstone. Her eyes, wide and dark, aim without blinking somewhere to the left of Paul Langman. Following her look, Paul Langman sees the man. He too stands still, locked in her gaze, clinging to it. Nothing for them matters—the world falling away—but their clinging to each other, their desperate love spanning the distance between them like a tensed arch.

Paul Langman seeks words to express this, but why? Who will listen?

It is a farewell, a last farewell, with a terrible certainty about it.

But why? Didn't the convicts say.... Paul Langman gropes about in his mind. The bath, the barracks—they are facts. The convicts are in good health, even well-fed, people around him point out. Yes, around him is relief. Practical people ask practical questions, trying to get information instead of careening on flights of imagination. Yes, practical, sensible people are relieved. And doesn't he also feel relief, considering the many barracks, and the convicts saying not to worry? And why would they say that, since otherwise they don't look like people who could be nice? That woman, she is frightened, and her man despairs for her, and he, Paul Langman, let his imagination soar.

Still he feels foreboding, and feels, when the woman starts moving, that invisible span between the two snap, and he feels that snap resonate through his heart.

"You'll meet them in the barracks," the convicts keep saying. "You can't bathe together."

He watches the woman trudge toward the officers, trying to fight off the memory of that woman's eyes. Then he sees the women move this way and that, somewhere further along the ramp. He can't see what is happening, but it flows at a slow, yet steady pace. Neither can he see the officers. The columns of women have come between him and them, and the dust rises high from under hundreds of feet.

The men just stand there, arranged in columns with the convicts forever telling them to "fall in."

The convicts, until now float somehow on the periphery of his vision and mind, although he does register what they do and say. The convicts are deportees, too, he learns.

They push ruthlessly, even hit out, and then drop comforting statements about hard work here in camp, but fair treatment.

There is something intriguing about them, and he will have to comprehend it so he can write it. Deportees too, they say. So it would be merely the striped outfits and their shaved heads that make them convicts. And yet.... Well, he will study them. One stands in front of his column. The husky man pays attention that they stand smart, and engages, simultaneously, in conversation with Mr. Schwartz standing in the next column.

"You said hard work, but fair treatment, right?" Mr. Schwartz asks, his voice sliding upward, his eyes searching the face of the convict.

"Right," says the convict, his head cocked, his eyes dark slits behind heavy folds.

"The women, the older ones, will they have to work?"

"Positively not." Very firmly. And then he says, "Of that I can assure you." His head stays cocked, his chin up, his eyes nearly closed now.

"And you said we'll meet the women in the barracks?"

"To the very same place you'll go," he says, his lips stretching then into a rubbery grin. And then a nervous twitch starts towards that grin, spreading until it reaches that grin, and until his lips tremble in convulsive ripples into a ghastly grimace. For a second only. Then his face turns into an empty mask.

Paul Langman feels short icy shivers run down his arms.

Two others come to talk with the convict, drawing him away, talking quietly and rapidly in a language Paul

Langman can't identify. The three convicts stand, very alike, and it isn't just their outfits. It's something about their stance and some subdued tension about them that makes them the same. The three then return to the men's formation and order it up the ramp.

The men trudge slowly and steadily, as had the women, and the dust rises under their feet and up around them as it had around the women. Somewhere along the way the five-in-a-column formation the convicts are anxious to maintain is rearranged into a single file. Paul Langman follows in that single file toward the officers who are visible again. Three officers stand in the midst of some regrouping. Some men are herded to the left, others to the right. Again they are lined up in five-in-a-column formations.

He too reaches the spot where the officers stand. The officer who seems to be in command wears a doctor's insignia. A handsome man, that one is, greatly at ease. A doctor, trained to heal—sworn to heal. Or do German doctors take the Hippocratic Oath, Paul wonders.

The doctor signals Paul Langman to move to the left. Another officer repeats the gesture. So Paul Langman moves to the left and lines up with the others already there.

There are no convicts this time. "Five in each column," says a young SS man.

And then Paul Langman sees clearly what is happening back on the ramp. The doctor faces the line slowly herded toward him, signals with the light elegant gesture as he had signaled to Paul. The two other officers repeat, if needed, the gesture. The men trudge to the left or to the right in accordance with the gesture.

The old go to where he stands, the rest to the other side.

But why?

Then Mr. Schwartz, again there, next to him, somehow always next to him, asks the soldier a question.

"Hard labor for them," says the soldier, pointing to the other group.

A blond young fellow is the soldier, big-footed, big-handed—a country lad.

"And for us?" asks Mr. Schwartz, again.

"Come on, Poppa, who'd expect hard labor from you?

"But then...."

"Why, don't the old deserve special care?" the soldier says, and then grins. It's a strange grin, hardly a grin at all, far more a baring of his clenched teeth, young, strong, close-set teeth. Then he guffaws in one brief, sharp little burst.

Paul Langman's heart begins to pound. Nothing like the husky convict is this soldier. Yet something is similar.... The grin? No. Terrible also, but uncomplicated. But what? Somehow the way he answered Mr. Schwartz, the words he used.... But then, suddenly, Paul Langman's mind goes blank and he just can't remember what or how the convict answered. Yet somehow he feels a dark specter of sameness between the convict and the soldier.

Then slowly the mist recedes and as his head clears Paul Langman remembers the answers the convict gave, and his face, and he knows that they are in on something, the soldier and the convict.

And Paul Langman also knows they are play-acting.

But why, he wonders. Nonsense, why would they?

Yet he knows they do.

But then, it can only be—God! What do they want us *not* to know? Rather, great Lord, what would they want us *not* to do?

A wave of nausea and dizziness sweeps over him. It seems to go on forever. But then it passes. Not completely, but well enough for him to hear the talk around him. "The soldier," people say, "is friendly."

Meanwhile, on the ramp the show has ended. Except for the three officers, the ramp is deserted. Those on the other side of the ramp are marched off. Other soldiers appear, come over to Paul Langman's formation, and start these men off too.

It is a brief walk to a building different in shape and larger than other buildings. They are herded into a long room. The room is dim and damp and has a strange smell clinging to it.

"Strip," bellow the convicts who have reappeared. "Strip," they yell. "Remember where you leave your things, so you can find them after the bath."

The room is empty.

"Where?" some ask.

"On the floor. Just remember where."

And, "Strip. Everything."

So Paul Langman strips, slowly, fumbling for some reason with each and every button, wondering how to express this, wondering who would believe him.

"Everything," someone hollers right behind him.

Startled, he looks up. It is one of the convicts. There are more of them, weaving their restless ways through the crowd.

Except one.

The husky man leans against the wall. His lips contort, twitching as they had at the ramp, but the twitch does not stop there, but shakes his entire face. He seems oblivious to everything around him, far away and alone in a dark and distant land.

But then another convict steps to him and tells him something. At that, he comes back from wherever he has been, draws away from the wall, and he too bellows, "Everything!" His voice crackles, his face still twitches. "Everything!" he yells, louder than the others while perspiration runs in hectic little rivulets down that twitching face.

And things fall into place at the sight of that face: the words behind the words—of the soldiers and of the convicts—of the rumors, and of that strange smell that clings to the building. And from that stillness inside Paul Langman, something emerges—a clear, sharp cut across everything. The future—forever inside him, forever part of everything—is gone. Felled. A void. Very tangible.

So that's it, he thinks, that's what it's like.

But here is no panic, no fear. No words. Here is quiet.

He wonders why.

He knows it is a strange quiet for him alone. It flows into him, soaks him and all he sees.

For a hot terrible moment fierce pain strikes him. Then that strange quiet returns, and he knows: For some reason this is what he is—the vessel into which things pour. This is why he is on this earth.

They can't take this from him. It will stay with him until....

He pulls himself up, watching his own body become straight and stiff. Inside, his strangely quiet heart stands still as though not to disturb with its beat this awesome moment.

And now he takes it all in with that clear, wonderful, terrible perception: the dim, narrow, low room with its rough walls, floor and ceiling, containing them in its damp, close confines; the Germans, lined up along a wall unbroken by windows, their legs astride, their young faces void of light; the convicts, tense, striped phantoms, their eyes looking into nothing, their mouths open in continuous bellowing; and they for whose sake these Germans have come from distant parts to face them here in this room, in this hour.

They, for whom all this is arranged.

They undress. Bit by bit their bodies are emerging from under layers of crumpled clothing.

"Everything!" the convicts bellow.

So they strip. Until neat little heaps of clothing dot the floor, until the room turns into a mass of old, waxy bodies, until people he had known throughout his life have turned into strange apparitions he can hardly recognize. Their familiar faces hover above their never-before-seen pale bodies, above folds of heavy flesh or above bony skeletons covered by wrinkled parchment.

So they strip. And they turn this way and that. Shaky, spotted, wrinkled hands cover shriveled testicles. Faces are shiny with sweat; eyes wide, bewildered.

Why, God? Paul wants to cry out, because for them he would scream, for them he would storm, for them there is no quiet inside. But the scream sticks in his dry throat.

For a crazed second, he wants at least to embrace them, to have arms long enough to take them into one loving grip.

But all he can do is tremble inside each of those naked bodies.

Next to him, Mr. Schwartz says something, chatters away. Paul Langman notices. He doesn't get the words.

They are herded towards a door. Mr. Schwartz stumbles. Paul Langman puts his arm around his shoulder, feeling all along it the dryness of Mr. Schwartz's skin.

When they reach the door his heart begins to thump. Afraid? he asks himself. Where has the quiet gone? He swallows hard, then draws a deep breath.

Inside him the quiet returns.

He enters the chamber with his arm still around the shoulders of Mr. Schwartz, the person.

Crickets Would Sing

"...and on summer nights we would sit in the garden, and the crickets would sing," says Kati.

There is silence after that. Eva, the smartest kid in school, perhaps in the whole town, doesn't say anything. Marti watches Eva and Kati as they squat in the bunk, not looking at each other, but somewhere far away.

"But crickets don't sing," Marti finally says. "They rub their wings together. Everybody knows that."

"Oh, for heavens sake!" says Eva, suddenly her snappy self. Of course she knows crickets don't sing, even Kati does, but for some reason it doesn't matter. "It's beside the point," says Eva. It's foolish, Marti thinks, to feel she could know any better than Eva and Kati. If they say something wrong and silly, somehow it always sounds true.

Still Eva and Kati are her best friends. Remember when that girl in the next bunk yelled at her? Well, she won't again, not with Eva around.

Fact is, she's lucky to be with them in the same barracks, in the same bunk, even standing in the same column at head counts.

Also, both of them know her mother, her father, and Marika, her little sister, and she knows their families and both of them come to her birthday parties, and she goes to theirs. Other than her own party, the last party she went to was Eva's thirteenth birthday party.

On that first night in camp after the soldiers had lied to them and then they couldn't find their families, Eva had said....

No, it wasn't that first night. Maybe it was the next day? It wasn't the next day either, because Eva just crouched on the bunk the whole next day and the day after that and she didn't say a word. So it was some other day she had said their families were all right. Now Eva would know. She can figure things out here just like she could at school.

She, Marti, cannot. It is all so strange: the camp, the barracks, the Barracks Elder and her Helps who yell and hit. Eva even understood what those girls who have been here for weeks had said. Eva said after she talked with them, "The other camps are better." And she said, "Our families are there. And the war will be over in no time, and they will be set free and they will go home."

"When?" asked Marti.

"Soon," said Eva.

"How soon?"

At that Eva got mad. She can get mad real quick. But then they made up, and Eva said it would be very soon, and all they have to do is hang on.

Come to think of it, that is what she always says.

But even Eva cries, doesn't she, like anybody else. Of course, Marti thinks, here crying is all right, not like at school where she worries about what other kids think. So, here even Eva cries and picks quarrels—and for no reason. Eva is just like other girls, sometimes nice, sometimes mean. But then she says something so funny they laugh or she says they should talk about what it would be like when they go home.

Kati is good at telling how they will arrive home, open the door, and there everyone will be—parents, family, just like before—and they will hug and hold each other. And then they will eat. There will be food! Kati describes that too—all that food.

So they talk between head counts. At least they did before the day that girl from the other bunk came over.

Here, they were, squatting on the bunk—Marti, Eva, Kati—when the girl sat next to Eva and whispered in her ear. And she went on and on, but only Eva caught a word of it.

Eva just sat there, listening to the girl. Then she said, "Nonsense."

"What did she say?" asked Kati.

"Nothing," said Eva.

"Don't you believe it," she said to the girl. "Not a word of it."

"Don't believe what?" asked Kati again.

"Oh, shut up!" screamed Eva.

Then, just a second later, she said, "I'm sorry, Kati." And she cried.

Now that's Eva for you.

Then she stopped crying and said the Barracks Elder and the Helps are mean, and no one should believe anything they say. So the girl must have told Eva something the Barracks Elder or the Helps said.

But why didn't Eva say what it was?

And since then, between head counts Eva does not stay on her bunk, but sneaks from bunk to bunk, which could get her slapped by the Barracks Elder and the Helps.

But Eva doesn't mind. She goes here and there and talks with this one or that one. She has gotten even snappier than before.

The whistle blows for afternoon head count and Marti has no more time for thinking.

Out in the yard, in formation, she stands behind Eva and in front of Kati. It feels good to stand between them, Marti thinks, and she always will. It doesn't matter whether crickets sing or rub, she decides. If Eva and Kati want to believe crickets sing, it's perfectly all right with her.

Then she forgets about their squabble as her feet get numb and stiff. Do they stand two hours? More? Even Eva can't tell how long.

Finally, the whistle blows, and they return to the barracks.

At the door a hand, like a vise, locks around Marti's arm.

"You there, stupid," says the Barracks Elder, big in her striped dress.

She drags Marti into a small room just inside the Barracks door.

The room is built like a huge crate, with three bunks, a splintery table and a stool inside.

"See that bucket under the bunk? And that rag? Wipe the table first, then the stool. Then wash the floor. Do you hear me?"

"Yes."

"You better wash it good," she adds, then throws herself on one of the bunks and stretches out.

Marti wipes the table, the rag flopping like a dead toad in her hand.

"Squeeze that rag, stupid. The table won't ever dry if you soak the damned thing."

Marti squeezes the rag, wipes the table, then the stool.

"There's a spot under the table. Make sure you get it."

Marti crawls under the table and scrubs. The Barracks Elder belches, sneezes and rolls to her right, then to her left.

The door is thrown open and a woman comes in, an Old-timer, for sure, like the Barracks Elder, with hair almost to her shoulders. She has a folder under her arm and wears a dress her own size. Even her shoes fit.

That is what Marti sees best as she kneels there—the woman's shoes, the left one tapping fast on the floor boards.

"Why, you sure have it made, Hilda, don't you?" the woman says. "Nice and cozy. Even a maid."

The Barracks Elder gets off the bunk.

"Hello, Herta," she says.

"A maid cleaning up," says the woman, "while madam lounges in bed."

"Want it, Herta? You can have it, the whole stinking job. I'm working myself crazy, worrying myself to death with these...."

"Working yourself crazy?"

"Sure, with stupid, spoiled brats. This very morning at head count—There are three hundred seventy-three, when there should be three hundred seventy-four. So back I run. The SS bitch is already counting Barracks Seven. Sure enough, one brat's under a bunk, fast asleep, not for the first time either. I'm telling you, every head count is a nightmare, and I'm working myself crazy, as I said, and...."

"Are you sorry now you wanted the job when it came open? Well, you won't have to work yourself crazy much longer."

"What do you mean?"

"The trains have stopped."

"So?"

"Come on, Hilda, you didn't think they would keep kids between ten and fourteen?"

"They have so far."

"Sure with the trains rolling in, and all the old people and the small kids and the chimneys too busy. It's a question of capacity, see? So they stored them, in your care, in good hands."

"They might have a new policy now, don't you think?"

"No new policy. The trains have stopped, so the capacity problem is solved. Now they'll be able to take care of your brats."

"Do you *know*, Herta, or do you *think*?"

Without a word, the woman takes the folder from under her arm, opens it, gives it to the Barracks Elder.

Stay in formation tomorrow morning after head count, it says.

"That could mean many things," the Barracks Elder says.

"You don't really think that, do you? You know what it means."

"Mop up?"

"Mop up."

Marti stirs.

"Get out, you stupid ass!" the Barracks Elder screams, grabs Marti by the arm, and flings her against the door. Then she pulls Marti back, opens the door, flings her out and slams the door.

Slowly, Marti walks down the aisle back to the bunk. Kati sleeps. Eva perches on the edge of the bunk. Marti climbs up and settles next to her.

"Cleaning?"

"Yes."

"Went fast."

"She didn't let me finish."

"How come?"

"She screamed, then threw me out."

"Why?"

"I don't know."

"What did she say?"

"She said, 'Get out, you stupid ass.' I was washing the floor and they both were standing there and...."

"Both?"

"The Barracks Elder and a woman who showed up."

"One of the Helps?"

"No. Some other woman."

"Old-timer?"

"Sure. She has hair and a dress that fits, and good shoes that fit too. Tan shoes. Comfortable shoes with laces."

"What did she want?"

"I don't know."

"But what were they doing?"

"Just talking, and there was that spot on the floor and I was trying to...."

"But what did they say?"

"Let's see. The woman called the Barracks Elder 'Hilda.' 'Hilda, you won't have to worry yourself to death anymore,' she said."

"Why would the Barracks Elder worry herself to death?"

"Because someone was under the bunk, and she had to run back into the barracks, because the soldier woman was coming."

"So it's the head counts. What did the other one say?"

"You won't have to worry anymore."

"Did she say why?"

"Because they will be taking care of us."

"Taking care of us how?"

"I didn't really get it. They were talking, just talking, and there was that spot. They must have spilled something...."

"Marti, think. What did the woman say about taking care of us?"

"She said first they took care of the others."

"Who?"

"Old people and small kids."

It seems that satisfies Eva because she falls silent. Marti stretches and yawns, then thinks, Isn't that good news? Someone will be taking care of them! So they should be happy.

But Eva just sits, and is not happy at all.

There is no way to figure Eva out. Not ever.

In fact, she looks funny, kind of gray.

"How did the woman put it?" Eva asks.

"I don't know. They just talked about all sorts of things like trains."

"What did they say about trains?"

"Well, the woman said the trains stopped. So now they can take care of us."

"The trains—now wait a minute. Marti, try to think, what exactly did she say about the old people and the small kids."

"She said they had to take care of them first. But I already...."

"Did she say anything else, right before or after?"

"It's hard to remember. Yes, she said something about chimneys."

"Chimneys?" she asks, her voice squeaky.

"She said the chimneys were busy and now they aren't. What did she mean...."

"Marti, try to remember. How did she put it?"

"'No more capacity problem with the chimneys,' that's how she put it, and I can't...."

"Did she say anything else?"

"She said they'd mop up tomorrow. What does that...."

"Mop up?"

"Yes, mop up. After head count. Eva! What's the matter with you?"

Eva crumples like a rag doll tossed into a corner. Beads of sweat form on her forehead and roll down her face.

Marti wakes Kati and they say this and that. They try to make Eva lie down, but she won't. She just sits there shivering.

Kati puts her arm around her, and so does Marti, and the three of them sit quietly.

Suddenly Eva starts to cry. No, not cry. She squeaks funny, creepy sounds.

"Talk to me, Eva," says Kati.

Eva won't. She just squeaks, her face pressed against Kati's shoulder. Marti can only see the back of her shaved head.

After a while, Eva stops, sits up straight, looks at Marti and looks at Kati.

She opens her mouth, her mouth gray and trembling, then closes it.

"Talk to me, Eva," says Kati again.

Eva will not. She just keeps staring at them, then she looks away. She says not a word for the rest of the afternoon. It's creepy when Eva doesn't talk.

When it gets dark, they arrange themselves tight against each other for the night, and then in the darkness Kati begins to talk about birthdays. She likes to do that. She says they will be home for her fourteenth birthday, coming up in October, and that she wants to invite them. She says she hasn't been at a party since Marti's in February five months ago. "It was a great party, Marti's party," says Kati.

At that Eva speaks.

"A wonderful party," she says. "I shall remember it as long as I live."

Then, after a while, Eva asks, "Marti would you like to put your arm around me?"

Marti does. She feels drowsy and warm between the two of them, with her arm around Eva—and Eva even asked for it! Eva remembered her birthday party and said she would remember it as long as she lives—Eva, who has been invited to so many parties.

Well, as Kati always tells her, she will be home by her next birthday.

Commandant Einer's Decision

Half-shaven, Commandant Einer pours a schnapps. It burns, until that pleasant lightness floats into his brain. He continues shaving, chiding himself for thinking too much. Where are his ideals, his commitment to the Party? The rallies, the parades, the standards glittering in the sun and the banners like flames in the wind are just memories. Their steps hard on cobblestones, thunderous together, what an awesome new light it was.

The cologne stings his face. Just one more schnapps, he thinks as he pours, holds it against the light. "Prosit" he says and upends the glass. Yes, the revolution has been good to him. He's not a mailman like his father struggling with the mailbag. He's an SS Commandant. He misses the Front since his leg was shot; thankfully, he can still do this tough, but necessary work. He must remember this, he thinks, and pours another schnapps, standing at the window, looking over the camp.

The camp looms, gray and stark in the harsh light like a stretch of badlands on a winter morning. Commandant Einer belches, his breakfast like sawdust in his stomach turning suddenly and torturously, as he watches the scare-crows below his window. This Selection has to be done, seven hundred wretched women to be inspected and the ugly SS women appeased. Commandant Horcke requisitions the sick for execution as though Einer is no more than a store clerk. And the factories are insatiable. "We need more. We need stronger ones," they order. He's a fighting man, not a delivery boy.

The forms lie on the green felt desk blotter. "One hundred and twenty-one" is typed on one. So that's what it will be, he sighs. It's time to start. The prisoners are in formation as he watches bowlegged Lieselotte prance in her SS culottes and boots. If they would just leave me alone, he thinks, as he walks through the gate and to the barracks.

Three months ago, after his first Selection, thanks to a bottle of schnapps he devised his method. That first Selection was a nightmare. "Those unfit for work," the requisition order said. His stomach was tied in knots, his throat dry as he struggled to inspect closely seven hundred women. From afar they looked like scarecrow puppets, but close.... What's so strange being close to them? For starters, he could actually hear them breathe. They smelled of sweat and chlorine, stale and damp. Most likely, it was their funny big eyes.

What a job that was. By the end of the formation he had not selected enough to fill the order. They all looked equally bad. How could he decide which should go? So he had to start over and Lieselotte smirked that crooked smile, anxious to tell Horcke. He was too meticulous. From then on just a quick glance would decide. He wouldn't look above their shoulders. The boniest would go. Simple.

Be decisive, he thinks, standing stiffly as Lieselotte fusses and announces all seven-hundred-fifteen are present. She had already leaked to the Barracks Elders those selected would just be sent to another factory. Little do they know this may be one of their last days on earth. Lieselotte is a crafty manager, so he has more time for the damned paper work.

Ninety-six are sent to the gate quickly. So efficient, he thinks while pulling the ninety-seventh exactly as he had planned, grabbing her sleeve, his eyes focused on her scarecrow arms. She goes to the gate.

As he turns to the next column, he feels a light, brief touch on his arm. When he turns back he sees a prisoner standing outside the last column, her hand that had dared to touch him flopping back to her side.

Her face is anxious. "Herr Commandant, please," she says and stares at him with wide eyes. A child, he thinks, although he can't tell how old they are. Why hadn't the doctors selected her in the beginning? Selection is a job for a doctor, not a soldier.

"Herr Commandant, please, she's my sister," the prisoner says pointing to the ninety-seventh girl, standing by the gate. Her sister, bigger, with a long gray face, waves her away with a shaky hand. "My sister," she says again.

"We would, Herr Commandant...." He sees her swallow hard down her thin neck. "We want to stay together, please Herr Commandant, my sister and I," she says looking into his eyes. "Please let me go to that other factory."

Jesus Maria, he thinks, and the words shock him this time, remindful of something long ago. But he catches himself forgetting his responsibilities while looking into her eyes. There's no time to think. He needs to act, as duty requires.

But she does look unfit, her sticklike arms, her neck like a plucked chicken's, her face smaller than his hand. Order her to the gate, you idiot, he thinks.

It's a scandal, his standing like a fool, ignoring his duty. With the prisoners, Lieselotte and the guards staring at him, he can't panic. He hasn't done anything noticeably wrong so far, and only seconds must have passed. He must act now.

But he can't. It's an awful fact. He swallows, yet his mouth stays dry. Is he mad? Then, like a life ring thrown to a drowning man knocked by waves, the idea hits him. He will act as if he is ignoring her, as an SS commandant should do.

He turns away with a jerk, hitting in haste his stiff leg badly against the other.

He hears himself exhale.

"Herr Commandant...."

Flames shoot through him. She won't shut up, the accursed fool. She won't let him.... Let her choke then, spit out her life in gasping agony; let her burn.

He turns and grabs her, flings her. She stumbles against her sister, then straightens, clutching her sister's hand, and breaks into a smile stretching across her funny mouse face.

"Thank you, Herr Commandant," she says.

His arm swings out before he realizes it. He grabs her and thrusts her back into the formation.

"But, Herr Commandant," she cries, childlike and bewildered.

The world spins drunkenly.

"Herr...."

"Shut up!" he hears himself scream and reaches for the other one and flings her back too, then turns and starts off, floundering in hot waves of dizziness across the yard, towards the gate. He needs to escape.

And then he sees Lieselotte, standing by the gate, her eyes narrowed like slits, her lips pursed.

Commandant Einer halts. So does the whirling world. Dense, hot silence soaks the yard, and Lieselotte stares, grim and dark, and behind her on both sides of the gate stand the guards.

He feels the sweat bead on his brow. He turns sharply, stalks back to the formation, reaches for the small one and then for her sister. "To the gate," he bellows, "both of you." Then he steps sharply to the next column, and to the next, and on and on, until those who stand at the gate number one hundred and twenty-one.

The

Praegner

Theory

Alfred Praegner sits with his back against the barracks' walls, his legs stretched on the dusty ground, wondering whether he might have hit upon a new conception of after-life. There is no purgatory, no heaven, no hell—or rather, not the deserved fire-and-brimstone hell of fiery preachers, and not the well-ordered, deserved, hell of Dante. There is no underground world like Hades, also known to have justice. Instead this general afterlife metes out its horrors haphazardly. It has no forgetting, but a strange remem-brance of life, life like a wondrous painting: detailed, lucid, clearly designed, and with a new, matchless understanding of perspective permeating every particular. This painting is studied, longed for, cried for, from this place indiscrimi-nate, this place for all: for saints, for villains, and for those in between, amongst them one Alfred Praegner.

Surely, this is a marvelous new theory of afterlife—the Praegner Theory, he thinks, then laughs. He stops laugh-ing, and draws with his forefinger a funny little face in the dust, wipes it away with his palm.

It must be around eleven, he thinks, looking up at the searing sun, white-gold and piercing his eyes.

The Praegner Theory...it will make him immortal, no doubt. He laughs again, then realizes he will have to share the credit for this extraordinary insight with the sun, the sun bearing down on his shaved head—skull, rather—making him lightheaded, making his mind take strange trips.

But then, maybe he should share the credit with some-thing less august than the sun—his empty stomach, its unfulfilled cravings affecting his mind.

The stomach idea is less flattering than the sun idea, he thinks and laughs again.

He laughs easily, but it is a new kind of laugh, not the kind he had practiced while alive. Alive? Yes. He used to be alive and is now dead.

According to the new Alfred Praegner theory he is dead, and the concentration camp is a stupendous innovation.

He wishes he could escape the sun. But he can't. So he stands, stretches his legs, flexes his muscles, then sits down again in the dust.

Don't escape, he warns, and then he lets go, as he does whenever he can, and wanders into that marvelous painting that is the past, or rather, like life. The streets, houses, trees, of this painting grow around him until they become life-size. He walks along a street, passes houses sharply defined against a clear sky, houses he has so many times passed. It is a simple street with simple houses, but there is that crisp, newfound beauty about it that makes it so novel, such a discovery.

Then the store window.... Was it that beautiful? Glass.... such a marvel! Shiny, cool to the touch, smooth, with a pleasing hardness. Just a store window, he tells himself, but knows it isn't really so. Like everything, it is a marvel— overlooked, never really seen. There is the door—more glass, also wood with peeling paint of strange patterns worth studying. There is the tinkle of the bell and inside he is. There is the smell of old paper; of fine, powdery dust; of leather bindings moldering away slowly, irrevocably; of wood, old, very dry. Yes, all that, and more too. Just what is there about the smells of old bookstores that defy definition...and time?

Books are stacked in nooks, in niches, on shelves, on tables, their colors clashing, vying, harmonizing. In the

back of the store stands a brass lamp with a glass shade—
old, ornate, the brass dark, the shade dust-gray-orange—
next to armchairs, leather of course, wrinkled and cracked.
They are creaky and incredibly comfortable. Between the
chairs stands a table piled high forever with books. Oppo-
site is a desk.

The setting.... Empty as yet.

But then a man sits at the desk, materialized in a
second. He has a medium build. His hair is neither dark
nor light. His age? It's hard to tell—and from here, of no
consequence anyway.

Rather nondescript, thinks Alfred Praegner, as he
draws a sad little face in the dust.

But then, he thinks, that man does look right, does
seem to be part of it all, there at that battered old desk, that
beloved, cluttered, ink-stained desk. Just like the woman,
materialized too, in the armchair nearest the desk. Of
course, she could not be called nondescript, now could she?
Even by someone else. Well, most likely not, but surely not
by him, her brown hair shiny and her eyes blue, light blue,
especially when she would look up. Yes, for some reason
then her eyes would look lighter blue, much lighter. Later
on they would be immense, he remembers, in her sick nar-
rowing face in those last months, seven years ago.

For a second it hurts as it did then, seven years ago, the
pain, wrenching and terrible, but then it passes. He sees
her sitting there as before—smiling, stirring her coffee,
her ever present coffee.

And so it would be, the moment in the painting: the
man at his desk, the blue-eyed woman in the armchair,
smiling at the man. The man smiling back.

There would be other figures in the painting, brows-ing in the background or seated in the other chairs, but not in the foreground. They are fine in their own right, but not the main figures of this particular painting, although still important. He then thinks guiltily about having placed them in the background. But things could be corrected, justice easily done, figures moved forward in remem-brance of past moments.

What a strange view it is from here, thinks Alfred Praegner, and what strange power I have.

The sun is right over his head. The dust is gray, the barbed wire fences twinkle in the sun, and the guard in the watchtower, with his hand on the machine gun, gazes down on the camp grounds.

Of course, this is not real, thinks Alfred Praegner. *Of course,* this place does not exist. Why would they make such a place for the likes of Alfred Praegner to sit bare-skulled in the dust in the sun? Why would they build fences, watch-towers to guard Alfred Praegner and his kind?

What is real is that simple street and that store and the blue-eyed woman smiling at the man at the desk.

That man. Nondescript, surely. Everything achieved by that man was in that small store with its signs, "New and Secondhand Books," and "Feel Free to Browse."

But then, people did come and browse and they did come back again and sat and talked, and there was the smell of books, and the store was warm. And late into the night the hair of the blue-eyed woman would shine under the light of the old brass lamp with its funny shade, while outside the soft, dark quiet would envelop the simple street of which the store was so much a part.

It was all right, thinks Alfred Praegner. It was all right. And he smiles quietly as he sits there in the dust.

Madam's

Career

When the elegant Herr von Hiltz promoted me to Supervisor because of my excellent work, the other machine operators were shocked. Their jaws dropped when he said, "I have ordered your Supervisor's smock, *Madam*." Only in this country would someone from a poor family like mine be able to be a Supervisor. He said the other workers were being moved. So I wondered who I would supervise.

"Prisoners have been requisitioned," he told me. "Jews from Hungary." I gasped. I had never seen Jews before. I should train them, but not talk with them. I should watch for sabotage.

I couldn't wait to write my first report so he would know he promoted the right person. How lucky I am to have a career.

Before the prisoners started last week, the stools were removed from the work area to prevent loafing. Fourteen prisoners operate my seven shell casing machines. I made the one who speaks German the interpreter.

The SS girls march them from camp. The SS girl in my area only has to watch from her platform and look smart in her culottes. I'm the one who has to work, but I look just as good.

These dangerous women wear rags and smell bad. Their hair is shaved; their faces are dirty.

Beanpole operated my old Machine Number Three, feeding the casings. Her friend, a crazy-looking girl with a clown face sat on the floor packing the sorted two-centimeter casings expelled from the machine. They were fifteen years old like me.

Mom is upset I bring an apple each day for lunch. We don't have much food and the prisoners crave what little we do have. Clown always stared at my apple when I ate. She swallowed every time I swallowed, even though we fed her plenty.

My work is exhausting. I'm working twelve hour shifts. Around four o'clock last Sunday morning when I caught myself starting to doze, I saw Beanpole wink at Clown, and throw back her shoulders, pull in her chin and make a funny face. Clown grinned, winked back.

I yelled at them for fooling around. But Beanpole just stared and Clown blinked stupidly, so I called the interpreter. At least she ran over like she should.

"Tell her to get to work," I told her.

Beanpole liked to lean her hip against the crate so she could show off by standing ramrod straight. I told her not to lean. She listened, looking at my chin rather than at the interpreter. Do I have apple on my chin, I wondered. The interpreter blushed when Beanpole answered her. "She said she understands, Fraulein," she said.

Afterwards, Beanpole still stood like a sentinel, even when I was near, just to taunt me. Last night Clown was crouching funny and casings were heaping around her.

"She's sick," said the interpreter.

"Malingerer," I said.

Sure enough, she got busy then, but soon slowed down again. Beanpole ran back and forth trying both to feed and to clear the machine causing confusion. I yelled. Beanpole opened her mouth as if to say something, but just shook her head in disgust and went back to her place.

"She was trying to help the small one catch up," said the interpreter.

"Tell her to mind her own business. I'll report both if she moves."

The real problem was I didn't know how to file a report. And I didn't know how I could report her without looking ineffective.

———————

Sunday afternoon, I learned that to report a prisoner, I need to write down the number tattooed on the arm, together with the offense and submit the form to the top office. Then I watched and waited for something to report.

Around ten o'clock, Wednesday, Clown coughed up blood spattering the floor, the crate and my old machine. Beanpole left her station no matter how much I yelled. So I called the SS woman. She slapped them silly and kicked Clown as she crouched on the floor. It didn't do any good so she was hauled away. I was anxious to report Beanpole for leaving her place and for not obeying orders but the SS woman said she would do it. She phoned for a replacement and one was brought over fast. Beanpole washed up the mess grudgingly.

———————

Beanpole came today with her face black and blue, one eye swollen shut, the other half-closed. I asked the SS woman if she had reported her because after all, I am a supervisor and just as German as she is.

"Can't you tell?" she said.

Around lunch time I was eating my apple and without thinking, walked over to Machine Number Three. Beanpole gave me an insolent look from her half-open eye. We are too soft, labor shortage or no labor shortage. How dare she not respect me.

"Absent minded?" she sneered. "Have you forgotten that thanks to you she will never be hungry again?"

I was furious, but then I realized she said it in German—even fancy German.

She had been mocking me all this time by making me call the interpreter. She mocked me by the way she stood, the way she ignored me, the way she stared at me when I spoke. She thought she was as good as me...even worse. I saw it in that half-closed eye. There was murder in that eye, but something else too—like she smelled something she had stepped in. How could I report her without looking bad myself? I puzzled over this problem for a while.

But then suddenly the solution came to me. I went to her machine and grabbed her arm hard while I wrote down her number, filling out the form carefully, writing, "She speaks German, but acts like she doesn't." I paid attention to my spelling.

———————————

"Speaks German, but acts like she doesn't," Erich, the handsome SS man, read aloud this afternoon as he sat erectly at his desk. "She must be removed," he ordered. "Surely she is dangerous."

Adjusting his red silk tie Herr von Hiltz said, "Your first report is excellent." Then he added with a proud smile, "*Madam*."

Red-letter Day

Anna Berger wakes early, as usual, and as consciousness comes back, she cries a bit. That too is usual. She weeps quietly, pressing her face against the straw mattress so as not to wake anyone in the bunks near hers. Crying is after all, a very private affair.

When it is over and that soft, lucid relief that follows crying comes over her, she begins her Morning Program. First, she says to herself, "Now this camp is not so bad—*really*. It's good to have a bunk to sleep in, to say nothing of having a blanket."

Next, she thinks of her work at the factory and tells herself she has been lucky with this assignment. Why, it has taken her less than a week to devise a method to operate that machine so she will not ache all over and still she can manage to get through the twelve hour shifts.

She works rather unconventionally. Surely she must look funny, a six foot tall, bony old woman operating a machine as though she were exercising. It is, after all, like an exercise—calculated and rhythmic. And it does work.

So that is the work and it's all right.

Really it is.

Then the girls who are her friends, Lili and Kati...but she shall perhaps leave thinking about them until the end of the Program, so she can have something pleasant to finish the Program, or rather, something pleasant to start the day. She likes to think about them and how she would, if ever free again—free? She stops and remembers now she dreamed she was free, this very night. That a thing like that should slip from her memory—even if only for a short time! But this is how dreams are. They come, then go—simply vanish—and then return at the most unexpected times.

But now, that will bring some changes in the Morning Program, because after she dreams that she is free, the day becomes, of course, a Red-letter Day, and in honor of that she may forget the Program and may try instead to recall the dream.

So she stretches out comfortably and closes her eyes. At first she just feels the mood of it coming back, the mood of unbearable happiness. And that would be all for a while, that mood. But then she remembers the rest: the garden, warm in the sun; the earth, fragrant as only in early spring; the breeze, cool from the river. And the sky, blue and clear.

Then suddenly, there's a strange sensation as though she were flying, high in that distant sky, soaring, like a bird. Light, she is, the air carrying her in a blue, translucent world.

That is the dream. Except for the soaring, it is much like other dreams she has when she is lucky enough. And as it comes back to her, she cries again. No, it is not easy, a Red-letter Day.

How can she continue the Program after that? Of course, she would have to if she would want freedom to ever be more than a dream. Or can she do anything about it, at fifty-seven? In this camp that's as incredible as being over one-hundred years old anywhere else. How long could her Luck last? What people call her Luck started with the Mistake, she thinks.

The Mistake. Back it is again, and once back, she knows it will bring back the rest as well—that first day and night in the other camp.

It was a summer morning, she remembers, nine months ago in June 1944. She and her transport had just arrived after five days cramped in boxcars. The bolted doors of the boxcars had just been opened, and she clambers down from one of them to the ramp below, stiff and shaky and blinded by the sunshine sharp after the dimness of the boxcar. The morning's dazzling sun bathes all in its relentless glare: the endless barren plain, the rows of barracks in the distance, the wires, the ramp and the crowd milling on the ramp buffeting her like big, dense waves.

She remembers clearly standing there, hearing her teeth chatter and trying to stop them. But she would never know whether she could or not because she remembers then the crowd, and her in it, flowing along the ramp, like a thick, churned-up river until squeezed into a single file by some Germans rushing back and forth among the crowd, busy, raging, red-faced. Then she remembers moving in that single file further along the ramp, and she notices the file diverges somewhere ahead of her. Then she reaches that point where it diverges, and she faces that officer standing there.

That officer—as though he had just dropped in from somewhere else—is elegant, his uniform marvelously tailored, a smart riding crop in his gloved hand. A trace of cologne wafts around him along with a tune he whistles, light, sweet, familiar, in three-quarter time. Just what is that tune, she wonders stupidly as she comes to a halt in front of him.

Then, with a light, nonchalant gesture of that gloved hand holding the crop, the officer points to the right, for her to go right it seems, for she feels someone pushing her.

So she moves to the right and lines up with others already there.

And then it gets terribly confusing as they are marched from there, with one thing following the other fast, and then finally there is that Girl—but that, of course, is later. The sun is low by then, shining straight into her eyes through the open barracks door and that Girl is standing with her back to the open door, to the sun. And she is facing the Girl, the sun in her eyes, her knees trembling, her head light, thinking this isn't happening.

All this shudders inside her like the memory of a frantic moment under water, black-green. She stands running her hands in dreamy disbelief, again and again, over her shaved head and the strange rags clinging to her still-wet body. Then, she thinks, it would be good to slip down to the floor, let go....

But she doesn't. She keeps standing there, watching that Girl as she stands in front of her, talking rapidly in a jerky manner, tossing out words one by one. And only the strange rhythm reaches her. She remembers clearly the effort to permit those words to enter her, and when they finally do, she tells herself: so that is what the ramp was all about.

And she remembers not feeling anything.

She finds herself squatting on the barracks' bare floor. She doesn't know how she got there, but there she is, enclosed by women heaving in restless sleep around her on the floor. Most likely she had slept, although, she couldn't really know. Anyhow, she squats feeling surprisingly alert. She tells herself again: so that was it on the ramp.

The Girl's words, like stones roll back and forth inside her. She has to stop them, and certainly can, now that she is alert. If she would just think it over, recall what the Girl told her.

So she would do that now, she decides, and tells herself there was a Selection on the ramp. She tells it as though she is explaining it to someone else. A Selection to live or ... she goes on, and that officer made a mistake. He should have sent me to the left instead of to the right. He was too busy, perhaps, with that whistling....

The Girl's words sound like the rules of an absurd game overheard in a mad dream. But it isn't a game and she has to understand it. So she starts over again. He should have sent me to the left, she repeats, slowly this time as though for the benefit of someone a bit slow. Because I'm old—that's why—not worth feeding. He should have sent me to be....

And then it dawns, but not through reason nor through understanding. She sees it in her mind, as though it were a movie—immense images flashing on a screen of naked, worn bodies, close, closer, in a bare chamber, a window-less sepulcher. Those bodies press against her own, the air thickens as the doors close—as that Girl had said it would—and then stinging fills the air.

She springs up and scrambles in the darkness over the sleeping women. But there is no way out, just legs, arms, torsos, twitching as she stumbles over them and sighs and curses and cries; and finally there is the wall. She knocks against it, solid and endless.

But there would be a door, there has to be. Groping, falling, getting up, falling again, getting up again, she moves along the wall. And then she finds the door. She pushes it open and steps outside.

Outside is the floodlit night: the rows of barracks, ash-gray in the lights; the watchtowers, menacing skeletal giants; and the fence, stretching across earth, sky, maybe the very world.

She stands looking for a while, then slides down to the ground alongside the knotty plank walls of the barracks.

The earth is crumbly and smells of dust and chlorine. But it is cool, and she feels its coolness creep up her body. Then she feels the cool air stream deep down her burning throat.

Much later, calm, detached by then, she wonders. Why had the Mistake happened, the German pointing right, not left, to she who had no one waiting in this life: her life no joy, her death no grief, anymore to anyone? Her life lately is not more than a dream of something that had once been, but a life of no use to anyone, so why did the Mistake happen to her?

It is not only senseless, it is unjust. Her detachment disappears. Why? she wonders, bewildered. But then she laughs. So ludicrous is this thinking of sense, meaning and justice.

She laughs silently, shaking all over.

She doesn't know when she stops laughing, when that feeling comes that makes her press her back hard against the barracks wall, and makes her heart beat as though a big clock were beating inside, strong, defiant—the feeling that she, if no one else, would give sense, even meaning, to the Mistake.

The Mistake thrusts her into an unknown, lonely world, yet heady in its own incredible way, and with a frenzied urgency that drives her to decide that as soon as possible she will work out a plan so she can give the Mistake meaning.

The madness passes and she sits empty. Then comes another fit—what else could she call it—to be free, just once more, even if only for a second.

Then abruptly that vision returns, exactly as it first came: those images first, immense flashes—those naked bodies, that chamber. And at that everything else vanishes: dreams of sense, of meaning, of freedom.

———

Why does she devise the Program, the plan she decided to design when the madness of "giving the Mistake meaning" came over her? She does work out the Program a couple of nights later and has been following it ever since, even though she recognizes the absurdity of *her* giving the Mistake meaning.

Who is she to challenge, and then, in that madness, that defiance—to dare feel close, so close as though she could actually touch Him.

No, not that. She shivers and tells herself she did not have a sane moment that night. Everything she thought then was preposterous.

But if everything was preposterous so was the Program. So why does she do it? Because it suits her dream to be free? But isn't that preposterous too?

Lately it does not seem so. Something is in the crisp spring air of 1945, and it isn't just wishful thinking, not this time. Time is running out for the Germans; even they in the camps know—why so do the Germans, at last. So, considering what she endured in the first camp which was so much worse and considering she survived Selections at both camps.... That nonchalant officer on that first day in the other camp was just the first. There were others like him, some as nonchalant, others not—anyhow, considering she has been so lucky, if she could hold on just a little longer, it might happen—she might be free!

She would go home, back to that old house, lonely though, as it had been for years with just her in it, yet full of memories. Back to that house, to that garden, to the earth fragrant in the spring.

But if not?

She feels, as she always would at this point, everything inside her halt. She must think of something else quickly. For what have these nine months been but fighting off thoughts with thoughts one could bear, thoughts that would comfort.

So now she tries to think of something else. The girls perhaps? Lili, Kati, even Ida. They've been with her since that day they met in the other camp. Yet they are outside that strange world that grows inside her since that first night. They are with the outside dreams, doubts, much as she likes them. Or rather, she likes them because they are outside.

The girls are young and act like it, treating her sometimes as though she were even older than she is, one who needs to be cared for—and she has to let them do so. Then sometimes, just a second later, they forget her age and fool around in those rare light moments in the same way they fool with each other. Well, not exactly: there would always be a difference. It's hard to put a finger on it, but they would fool just the right way somehow.

Then there were moments. Once—now it is really strange why that felt so good. Ida one evening showed up and leaned against their bunk, smiling her sarcastic smile, and joked, "Now Grandma, how's it feel to be such a tall drink of water?" Both girls spoke up at once on her behalf but in such funny terms they all ended up laughing. And it felt so good somehow.

It was good for another reason, too. They put her in that happy mood. Sooner or later she would have lost her temper, as she always does with Ida. She could never learn to ignore petty things the way smart people do. So she says something petty herself and later regrets it. Oddly enough, the things that matter, she can handle.

———————

The whistle sounds, the lights go on. She says her prayers quickly, not the way she has said them since that first night, like a dialogue spoken by one person. Fact is, prayers usually take time, and today she has run out of time, so she prays quickly, then goes to the washroom.

Instead of the usual noise and chatter, the washroom is quiet. Guess it's too early for them. Chuckling, she thinks not everybody is as young and vigorous as she is. But when she returns to her bunk, she finds the girls huddled together with some others. They hush when they see her.

So then she knows.

"Well, girls, we wouldn't be scared by a Selection, would we?" she says.

And she isn't, or at least she feels so while she smoothes the blanket over her bunk and rushes to roll call, although she does catch herself talking too much, and maybe a bit too loud.

The roll call is held indoors because it's still dark and foggy. They line up in five long rows from the door at one end of the narrow building to the far wall, down the broad main aisle between the bunks. The string of bulbs swing from the ceiling above them as they stand after they are counted and wait for the Commandant.

Anna Berger stands midway between the door and the far wall with Kati to her left and Lili behind her, her breathing loud, labored and raspy. She begins to pray for the two girls then, or rather to beg. Then she thinks they are young and strong-looking. It feels good to think of that—just for a second though, because then another thought pushes it aside: What about me? She quickly tells herself she is strong-looking—that big, bony frame, of course, the only explanation of her Luck. Also, she doesn't look fifty-seven, as the girls always would say. "The Commandant would never guess," they'd say. Still, no one knows what might happen.

She must stop these thoughts, no matter how hard. For some reason today is even harder than other Selections. Maybe it is because no Selection has been held for nine full weeks. More women have been getting sick than ever, and they sure look sick, no matter how hard they try to look strong and healthy. The factory has taken its toll. Yet somehow things have gone on without Selections and replacements. It's just a delay. It's foolish to think the Germans might be losing.... But even just a delay is good: the later one Selection, the later the next, if there is a next Selection with the end so near. Every gained second holds a promise, vague and incredible, living in their minds, awake and asleep.

Time....Yes, even just a delay is good.

That's how she must look at it.

But now here it is—the Selection. Here it is, and the girls must have known. They kept it from her. God bless them, for it was a lovely night, with that dream, and it would not have been like that if she knew today she might—but no, she should not be afraid.

She watches the shadows shifting rhythmically into odd, ever-changing patterns between the bunks on the other side of the aisle, shifting in accordance with the perpetual swinging of the bulbs overhead. She thinks that by the time she counts to ten thousand the Commandant would come. She counts slowly. And then, because he is still not there, she tries to think of her dream. But that doesn't work. So she tries to think of something else. Of the old house, perhaps? But that doesn't work either. Then maybe about.... There is noise in the corridor, and the door is thrown open. But it's only the SS woman, the small one with the pockmarks. She pops in, then out again, like a clock's cuckoo. The door slams behind her.

Why isn't the Commandant coming? Maybe he's sick! Nonsense, she thinks. He's here, probably in the small office next to the gate. What would keep him this long? What does a man do before he selects people to be...? Probably, he would be attending to orders, or forms she decides. Surely, forms need to be sent with those transported to that other camp where they have the facilities—to handle those sent there. Germans are so bureaucratic. He would have paperwork to take care of first. On the other hand, he might just be sitting, tugging on his gloves. Or he might be pacing his small office and cursing and telling his assistant he prefers the Eastern Front, damn it!

Or maybe the whole thing will be called off!

No such thing has ever happened. Then maybe—

His steps are strong on the corridor boards. She hears them well before the door opens. He stops for a second at the threshold.

His face is gray. She can see it well, can see the muscles twitch above his jaw. Only when he comes nearer will his face grow fuzzy, she remembers, and then thinks, I need reading glasses. The idea seems obvious and natural. But its absurdity hits her, and for a second she fears she will scream.

He, meanwhile, walks to the first column of five deep and stands in front. Then he steps to the next. He reaches out for someone. That someone steps out of the formation. She is tall and stooped, and the bones in the back of her long neck stand out sharply as she stands in front of him. He motions her to cross the aisle. She goes. As she stands there, one of her stockings slip slowly down and settle in thick, gray and trembling folds around her ankle.

I wish I were blind, thinks Anna Berger.

There is another, a dusky, haggard girl; and still another, a wren-faced little woman; and then more and more as he steps from column to column and reaches out again and again.

Those on the other side of the aisle stand stiff, their heads held as though balanced with infinite care on their necks long and strained, their lips tight—bloodless streaks on ashen masks.

They stand as they always do, those on the other side, at each and every Selection.

And after each Selection, throughout the night, Anna Berger tosses in her bunk, wondering whether she too would have stood there stiff and silent, whether what had

been churning inside her—that dark, turbid animal—
would not have burst forth had she too had to join the line
across the aisle.

Why do they stand there like that? Is this some grasp
of self, tight, unrelenting, the last stand of pride, while
terror grasps body and muscles, grasp within grasp?

She doesn't know. Maybe she should discuss it, she
sometimes thinks, but she never does, never would. Nobody
has. Maybe it is better not to.

So she doesn't know, yet she wrestles until exhausted,
she decides it doesn't matter. Isn't this all that is left, this
macabre victory?

And she feels it is victory, even if macabre. Nothing
is left but this victory for them, or for her if...or maybe for
all of them, on both sides of the aisle. Nothing is left but
to die, if one has to, as something still one's own would
demand.

There are things they can't rob, she concludes, and
she feels as though she has prayed. Now there is only this
moment, the Commandant stepping closer and closer.

But then what she knows so well begins, the thing
she fights always without avail. She physically feels it, as
though a tight cap presses down upon her head jutting
above the others like a solitary mountain peak. But then
come her years. All fifty-seven of them become tangible,
as though she can actually touch each year as they crowd
threateningly, accusingly.

She clenches her fists, swallows hard, and tells herself,
the years are all that's left. That helps, as it always does,
a bit.

He keeps coming, at times slow and at times fast. She
sees the distance close between them, and then just four

columns are between them, then three, and then he is at the next column. Kati is in that column. She sees him stop in front, then step away. He passed her, she thinks. But all is a whirling haze, for he is in front of her column.

He stops, his face is fuzzy. Through the haze she feels his eyes pierce hers. His arm jerks forward. For a second it hovers in the air, then flops down, and he steps to the next column.

She feels as if she's been picked up by an immense wave and tossed into empty, suffocating heights, then dropped. Sweat breaks out. Her knees shake under the suddenly immense weight.

Then it is over and all becomes clear, as though etched in the finest lines: the Commandant, reaching now for someone; the five long rows of cropped heads, stretching to the far wall of the barracks; that row across the aisle, beginning near the door and growing one by one in the Commandant's wake. Between them and her are only a few steps across the worn floor boards.

All is clear, and she is outside it now, a mere spectator.

Then it happens, a commotion somewhere further down the formation. At first she sees just the Commandant's cap in the midst of the rows of heads. He enters the aisle, dragging a girl by her wrist.

The girl is young and strong and big. Why did he—but then, he has done that before, has been slow and meticulous for a while, then hurried and totally haphazard. They stand in that no man's land between those to go and those to stay, he grabbing her wrist and she balking, head lowered and pushed forward.

"No! No! No!" Her screams are sudden, shrill, inter-mittent and shattering. "Please! Please!" Her voice surges from her chest, all animal and thick.

The two stand frozen in the silence, the like of which Anna Berger has never heard. It is as though she were lying in her grave.

"Please," the girl screams into that silence. "Please! Please!" she begs, each one pitched higher, the last, the shriek of a frenzied beast, jolting Anna Berger's mind into a wild spin with a mad jumble of thought fragments, racing round and round: Program to go by...Mistake...that officer...all that's left...meaning...sense...the garden...the sun...a bird...but where...once, just once again...all that's left.

Then emerging from that crazy jungle, something.... No, God, not that!

She doesn't understand whatever is emerging. She refuses to understand. The Commandant has passed her over. Who is she to question God?

"Please...."

No, God, I won't, Anna Berger thinks with anger gushing up, black and blind. Hammer strokes echo within her that it's almost over, it's spring, 1945!

They stand, those to go and those to stay. She feels something in that hot, murky air encompassing her. Those she loves, loves with ferocity, stand on both sides of the aisle. The girl stands, her wrist in the Commandant's grasp, her neck bent forward, her mouth wide open.

No, God, I won't, Anna Berger tells herself, yet looks at the girl, the pale tense arc of her neck, then tries to recall what a mere moment ago she was holding onto. But she can't.

"Come," the Commandant bellows and pulls.

"Please," the girl screams and falls on her knees in front of him. And there is no knowing whether it is from the pull or from her....

"Herr Commandant."

The voice is taut, but clear, strange, as though the voice of someone else. But hers it is, and somehow she stands in front of the formation. The strange voice says, "Let me go instead."

She sees the Commandant stare at her, his eyes wide. She looks back into those wide eyes, and so they stand in the aisle.

"Let me go instead."

She sees him nod, sees it clearly, from far away though, for strangely enough she feels far away, and light, like a bird soaring in the sky.

Three Women

Irma is doing it right now. The baby won't feel any pain. And she will put it, small but perfect, among the other bodies, behind the barracks, piled one upon each other like driftwood. And there will be no pain. Irma will see to that.

The woman—I must tell her. Irma will not. "Not me, Doctor," Irma told me.

It would be done by now, with no pain.

The woman on the floor—I must tell her.

"Doctor...."

Is it me she calls? She lies on the planked floor, in the blood on the floor.

I have to tell her.

"Doctor.... Can I have my baby?"

Can I—what? Blood pools on the floor, and the woman lies in the blood, looks at me, her eyes gleaming.

"Can I have my baby, Doctor?"

She is young, and at the end it went fast, and then Irma said, "Boy," and she took him in her arms, and carried him from the room to....

"Doctor!"

Why is Irma taking so long? But then, she said I have to tell her.

So *I* have to tell her.

"Doctor! Lady! You there!"

I have to.

"Where's my baby? I want my baby! I want my...."

The tight, small, planked room—this bloody coffin whirls. The infirmary whirls. The camp whirls—barracks, fences, watchtowers.

A clean room. It stands still. Water is in the glass. And I can see through the water.

A pill. And dense white fog.

But then, again: The woman is on the floor, on the slimy, bloody floor.

"Doctor...."

My back is pressed against the wall.

"Doctor!"

The woman looks at me, waiting, and Irma is outside with the boy.

And again, confusion. Which room am I in? The planked, bloody room or the clean, quiet room or both?

I am in the clean, quiet room—the glass, the water. It is now, not then.

I will write what happened. Then. That will help.

May, 1944.

The woman comes to the camp infirmary. Six months pregnant.

Question: Why didn't the SS notice she was pregnant at Selection?

Question: Why don't they ever notice she's pregnant?

Answer: I don't know.

Fact: They don't notice.

Question: Did she know what the SS would have done if they had noticed?

Answer: I don't know.

Fact: I don't tell her what will probably happen to
           her. Instead, I tell her to hide behind the others
           at head count.

I tell Irma the SS will notice. They don't.

––––––––––

June—

The woman comes to the infirmary again. Seven months
pregnant.

Irma asks me, "What now?"

"Hide her in the storeroom."

"And then...."

Then, comes the night and the wait. The pain and the
pushing.

Fact: Baby was doomed from the beginning. Woman
is young and might survive....

Finally, outside the storeroom I whisper, "You have to
do this, Irma."

Irma says, "I will. But you tell her."

––––––––––

*I can see through the water. This room is clean. There is no blood.
This room is quiet.*

*There is no shriek, no jump to stifle her mouth shrieking like
a beast into the deadly night. And the woman's hand is not at my
throat.*

––––––––––

"He was stillborn," I tell her, but she does not believe me.

"But he cried...."

Then words burst inside that room, that planked, slimy, stinking coffin. Words...from me, the woman.

Finally, I say, "Yes, I did it. I had to. If not, you too would be...."

Then comes the shriek. Then comes the woman's hand at my throat.

Irma stops her.

And then quiet, in that coffin, in that room: Three women stare at each other. Three women.

———————————

A clean room. It stands still. Water is in the glass. And I can see through the water.

A pill. And dense white fog.

Another night.

To

New

Zealand

As Herta Norman stumbles through the forest, the flares fade, lighting finally only the dark sky and the sinuous gray trees behind her. I must have reached the ridge, she thinks, looking back from the clearing. She stops and listens to the firing, standing taut like a bow until her knees tremble and long, hot spasms run along her calves. The firing seems far away. She lets go and slumps, crouching on the ground.

She presses her hot palms on the cool ground and feels its coolness spread from her hands up her arms. She listens motionless between bursts of fire to her panting and the pounding of her heart.

She stands and takes off her prison coat, unwinds a raincoat wrapped flat around her waist, and puts it on. She shivers. The raincoat is too light. Where can she hide her prison coat in this barren April mountain forest?

The question seems all-important and unsolvable. But right away, it is unimportant; then important again. I am tired, she thinks. She sits, the warmer coat on her back over the raincoat. I have to think this through. No time to be tired. The very idea, worrying about a German search at the end of the war.

Still she has to dump the coat, also the number and marking on her dress sleeve. She reaches inside the rain-coat, just below her left shoulder. She tugs, feels the small, soft cloth pieces in her hand and slips them in her pocket. Then she realizes her dress is black and white striped. She has to keep the raincoat buttoned up, no matter what.

She feels a rush of panic for acting before thinking, for being dangerously tired. But then she thinks of the rain-coat. Long ago, when it made no sense, she had traded information for it. And now here it is—all-covering, unmarked. Same with the scarf. She knows she can wrap it around her head so that her luckily curly hair can peek out and not look cropped.

How well she planned. How well she speaks German and how lucky she is to have been born in a town just over the German border. Her easy, fluent German has served her well as the Barracks Elder.

But it's more than luck, it's smarts. Others speak German, don't they? Yet she was the only one in her barracks with the sense to make use of it. She needs to plan for when she finds a town. Planning during the march had saved her.

She had to escape the other prisoners, for sure, after that swine Commandant shoved her into the ranks with the barracks women when the camp was evacuated. But it proved lucky that he wouldn't let her march alongside their columns.

She kept thinking throughout the march, planning, weighing odds, so when the fighting caught up she would be ready. It happened suddenly, although not unexpectedly, because she just had to watch the jumpy guards as they gazed into the sky, searched from every height. So when the firing started at twilight, the guards and prisoners ran into the forest. She was ready.

Planning, a quick decision and good timing saved her. They will save her again. Her brains always work for her, tired or not. They are more reliable than people. She will eventually come to a village. She needs stories for any situation.

Think systematically. As to the first possibility: what if the Germans still hold the town? She is a refugee, she could say. A refugee from—let's say—Silesia. The country is full of refugees, even she knows that. That's a good story.

As to her sudden appearance from nowhere, her train was attacked. It also explains why she has no papers: They were lost in the confusion. She remembers a railroad junction next to the highway. That's it. There was a raid at the junction, on her train. She fled and got lost. Surely, that will do for the short time left the Germans, because whoever was shooting at the highway—the English, the Russians, or the Americans—will soon be at the junction, if not already. If they're already there, the second possibility, she will just unbutton her raincoat and remove her scarf.

It seems simple, but what if the German soldiers are still in the village and she should run into one of the camp guards? She shivers, then calms down, thinking the camp's SS will still be guarding the prisoners at the slope.

Besides, she will probably find the Allies. For a few minutes this idea is bliss, a dream. But what if she runs into some of the barracks' women? No, if freed, they will stay near the highway like sheep, happy and tired. Then she remembers the twilight, the confusion. What if one of them escaped like she had? None would have dared, she tells herself, but one might have and they might end up together in the same town. And if the Allies are there...but she can talk her way out of any situation.

She can't waste time worrying what might or might not happen. She has rested enough. She lets the coat slip off her shoulders. The ground slopes slightly down, so she walks more easily, yet more slowly because she remembers the branches that slashed her face. She keeps her left arm raised to protect her face, and gropes with her right hand.

The descent becomes steep. She is surprised when she steps into an ice-cold and swift brook. Its rock bottom is slippery. She has to struggle to escape even though it's shallow. She sweats and shivers simultaneously as she finally makes the bank and removes her shoes. She squeezes her wet stockings, shakes the water from her shoes, and puts them on. They're clammy and cold.

Damn the women, she thinks, the Germans and them, but she can't afford anger. Be aware. She has outsmarted them both until now, so she should be able to outwit anyone. Everything in life is a question of brains. Why else hadn't the other prisoners gotten along with the Germans? They had exactly the same chances hadn't they?

It was not about moral questions or hypocritical stuff. That tall fool marching next to her lied to the others when she said, "Herta would grab six rations of margarine." It was never more than three. And she deserved them. If that fool was in charge she would have done the same thing. What really made them want to kill her, it seems, was that stupid sick girl who would have died anyway.

The rest isn't serious. But that girl.... It's foolish to let that girl upset her. It's not easy, considering the trouble that girl caused by being sick, and that Herta had to consider her own future.

And the barracks' women still haven't gotten over that girl. She thought they had, because it wasn't a big deal, not compared to what the Germans have done. How mean is that— to judge her more severely than the Germans!

They even reprimanded the one who brought up the margarine. "Margarine?" the fool said. " Have you forgotten the girl in the hard-labor brigade?"

"Well, it's not a bad statistic," said another. "Just one out of three hundred."

That firing, the dusk and the forest were blessings. Who else had the wit to use those few seconds of confusion? So they are huddling like animals in a storm, unless the Germans have mowed them down. She need not worry.

The ground climbs then levels. She smells pines. Smooth needles soften the earth. She stops in the scented darkness. The forest seems strange. It's the silence, deep, dense, unbroken. The firing has ceased. It's not just a lull. She holds her breath and stands, feeling the quiet envelop her like an immense, heavy cloak. What can she use as a marker to guide her?

The silence sweeps over her, leaves her gasping.

She will relax, think it over and consider it. Then she realizes there is nothing to consider. She needs to wait until dawn and not chance running into them.

She sits, a tightly coiled spring, saying it's insanity to wander without bearings. She catches herself frightened again and again by the silence. After a while, she feels her muscles loosen. She fights sleep, sits erect against the tree and glares into the dark.

She wakes right away, or so it seems, startled by voices from behind. She listens with a pounding heart, but silence surrounds her. Is it a dream? Something rustles, then is silent.

She runs ahead. Dream or not, they must be near. She will know where to head. Her instincts are as sharp as her mind. She thinks while scrambling she will go to America. Maybe New Zealand.

It's an excellent idea, solving all her problems. But later, resting under a tree, she thinks it's foolish. She has already solved the stickiest problem, getting away. There will be chaos for some time, so even if the Germans don't mow the prisoners down in the last moment, even if they should be liberated, they won't track her. They will be occupied patching up their lives, dashing home in search of their families.

New Zealand? Ridiculous. She could go home. What has she done, after all, that won't be forgotten once tempers have cooled?

But, these women are vicious and vindictive. They will twist things. Still, one girl gone is nothing to what the Germans have done.

The ground grows bushy, uneven and she hears a brook. She feels her heart contract. Is it the same brook? She has been too confident. She stumbles over a stone, falls against something hard, a boulder. She stands quickly and the world rolls and heaves. She steadies herself against a tree and keeps repeating, "Pull it together." She breathes deeply, presses her back against the tree trunk and somehow it works. She has to remember the other brook. The ground rises near that brook.

She slides her feet along the ground, first one, then the other, still holding the tree. Letting go, she takes a few tentative steps. The ground is flat. So it's another brook.

Maybe not. It might be another stretch of that same brook. She should leave quickly. But her knees tremble, so she sits, afraid she will be dashing among the same trees all night. Then it occurs to her, right out of the blue: She doesn't remember her face—that girl's face. She was paler than anyone. She does remember that, but just that. She shivers.

Something hits the branches above her, swoops as though from nowhere. Something shrieks. There's wild thrashing. There's more shrieking, waning this time. Then something flies away, or does it? She just hears a wisp of air. Then silence returns thick and dark.

Herta Norman listens with her entire body, sensing some formless and dark presence. Then the thought strikes just like the bird: what if that girl had not.... What if she survived?

Sweat breaks over her body. She jumps up and runs. I hate her, she thinks, panting, feeling the cold air rush through her open mouth into her burning throat. I hate everything about her: her sickness, her paleness, her stupidity.

———————

Most of all Herta hates she has no face, just a pale blotch instead, a smudge. She wants to scream. I'll go to Australia, she tells herself, running. Or New Zealand.

She knocks against rough trees; roots reaching from the ground; branches, low and cutting; bushes, boulders and brooks.

Then she remembers: above the girl's left brow was a birthmark. She sees the birthmark clearly, but not her face. Just that paleness, vague and undefined, and that birthmark, but not her face. She won't recognize her. She has to watch everyone for a birthmark.

"I'll go to New Zealand," she shouts into the dark. She hears her screeching, thinned-out voice as though it's not hers, but some forest creature's.

———————

When it's over, she lies on the ground, saying the girl is dead, she can't possibly be alive.

She will go to New Zealand anyhow.

She lies quietly, her face against the leaf covered ground, dead leaves from a past year. She lies for a long time, breathing in their earthy, faintly sweet smell.

I

Shall

Dance

and

Teach

In the darkness she hears the gravel crunch under the heavy wooden soles of their boots. She trudges along, lifting one leaden foot, then the other. She had stuffed her boots with crumpled newspaper and laced the canvas tops carefully, even tied them about her ankles with extra strings, yet the boots live a cruel life of their own, loose in spite of all that paper, the solid wooden soles tilting, slipping on gravel, hitting against her sore ankles.

I shall dance and wear a white dress with a tight bodice and a full skirt, swinging, swishing and rustling because it will be silk, of course.

She decides to check her string belt. It's tight. There's no reason to keep checking it. Above it, inside her dress, spongy against her skin, the bread is secure. A nice chunk, the size of her fist, a day's ration. Well, almost.

My classroom will be full of light, and my students—how old will they be? What will I teach? I'll have plenty of time to consider that. What matters is learning to teach. I'll enroll in the university. I will teach bright, happy students in classrooms full of light.

I'll both dance and teach. I can't dance all the time. I can't teach all the time. I'll do both.

That's the marvel of life.

And there will be life now, surely.

She knows now, not just hopes. She has known since they were lined up near the gate five abreast, facing not the camp, but the gate, wide open. There will be life, within days, maybe hours....

What if at the last moment the guards...?

Please, God, no! I will live.

Five abreast—five backs in front of her, and five backs in front of those, and those, and those, like taut bows. If she touched one would it break with a twang?

Off the formation stood the Commandant, his face looking as if sculpted of putty by a crazed boy. At the gate, gray against the setting sun, were the guards.

So out they marched in the dusk.

―――――――――――――――

From the curve of the road, up on the hill, she had a last glimpse of the camp: gray upon gray—barracks, fences, ground; deserted and still. The door of the first barracks, the one nearest the gate began to swing slowly as though an unseen hand opened it, then pulled it closed. Did she really hear the hinges screech? She couldn't have possibly.

Then all vanished. The road disappeared in the thickened dusk. And of course life is at the end of this road and she should think of that, of a university where they will teach her to teach. Maybe she can enroll this fall. Only one year lost.

Gained, she sometimes thinks. If horror had to happen, at least she had seen it.

That's crazy. Maybe not, even if some think it's totally crazy or can't understand it, or whether she can really understand it, let alone explain it. A university would help her understand things. And until then, if it had to happen, at least she had seen it.

It sounds like she is a spectator. She certainly is not. And because of that she knows—now that's the wrong word. " Feels?" Better. Still, not right, but then what? How silly is this, toying with words on a German road in the spring of 1945, on the night of April 12. The world around is wrapped in black felt, the earth smelling like a freshly dug grave.

No! The earth smells like—like fresh furrows. Exactly, and life is teaching, dancing and much more.

A turquoise dress will go with my eyes. My hair will soon grow long again and swing around my shoulders like hair should.

She slips her hand carefully inside her dress, just above the string belt, between the two lowest buttons. She breaks off a bit of bread, walnut size, pulls it out carefully with her other hand cupped under it. She chews slowly, then slips her hand back, but pulls it out empty. Not now. Later. It's good to think about having something to eat.

"Why the devil did they evacuate us?"

"Why...are you crazy?"

"The Americans can't be far away. There's firing."

"That's an air raid."

"No, that's artillery."

"We have a military expert in our midst."

"It's the Russians. The firing's from the East."

"It's pitch dark for heaven's sake. How do you know where's East?"

"At the last minute the SS will...."

"Shut up."

"They will. They can't let us live."

Silence again. Just the crunching of gravel.

The SS.... Back it comes that scene on the ramp, as it has so many times since it happened in June 1944.

The SS man stands on the ramp, hands on hips. Not an officer, he doesn't have that sharp outfit, but it doesn't matter.

With a cube head and a cube body he seems built from blocks with his face etched into the top block. He stands in the sun next to the boxcars just opened, the jumble inside just revealed.

Wearing a mouse colored house dress, red-poppy colored kerchief and a huge, crumpled white apron, the small wiry woman stands for a second at the boxcar door, then sits to clamber down, but loses her hold and lands seated in the dust. The mouse colored dress puffs around her, her shoes like brown barges upended on a barren shore.

In silence, hands still on hips, the SS man surveys her. Then he backs off in an athletic way, stirring up the dust around his boots and makes a playful run towards her and kicks her.

Down the ramp she rolls, gray-red-white rag doll.

Why wouldn't they kill them at the last minute? They certainly could.

Oh, God, her crazy daydreams! Dancing, for heaven's sake. How could she dance? —but she could have told Rozsi this. "Rozsi," she would have said, "I have this daydream." Rozsi would have listened, the grave little line creased between her brows, her head cocked in concerned contemplation. She would not have questioned whether it would be right for her, or for them, ever again to dance. She would have just tossed one word first. She loved to do that. "Turquoise" she might have said, or "white," and then she would have laughed and said, "Sure, you should dance. Wear whatever color dress you want."

Yes, Rozsi would have said that and laughed.

What makes a laugh? Lips? The throaty sound? The twinkle in the eyes?

What happens to it after death? Rozsi had the same lips, muscles. What happened to her laugh? Was it buried with her gray skin, taut jaw?

God, why should they drag themselves down this accursed road, stay on this crazy globe?

"Dance," Rozsi would have said. "Dance for me too."

Yes, that's what Rozsi would have said. But would she have been right? Besides, no matter what Rozsi would have told her, would she ever be able to dance again?

Who is she, after all this?

———————————

She needs to take stock, on this road, this night.

First, her head. Cropped. She remembers, would forever, how the cold steel felt as it glided up and down her skull and how her hair lay silky and dead under the soles of her feet on the damp floor.

Then, her eyes. When had she last seen her eyes? But this doesn't matter, what matters is what her eyes have seen. But she won't recall on this evil road what her eyes have seen. Never again. She was crazy to have thought it was good to have seen this. It's a curse, or it would be if she lets it. But she will not.

Ghosts, even Rozsi, let them be. Rozsi would have understood.

Forget her eyes. What about this body under the striped dress with its yellow parchment skin, her legs and arms like driftwood. What if she stripped and faced a full-length mirror...White? Turquoise? Full skirt and tight bodice? Someone's arms around this body? Is she mad?

And if so, what about teaching and the marvel of it? Of life, dancing, love. Rozsi, you were lucky. I wish I were with you.

―――――――――

A dark village under a starless night and a blackout, of course. So totally dark.

This must be a street. Cobblestones are under their feet, crunching like flint stones. Houses sit back, pallid square shapes against the dark, sensed rather than seen.

Shouldn't the dogs bark?

So they live in these houses, these Germans, in this German village.

―――――――――

Gravel. Space surrounds them again and the smell of dry, crusty soil.

"Was that a village?"

"It was a graveyard. Didn't you see the tombstones?"

"They were houses."

"What's the difference?"

"What do you mean?"

"The Germans, dead either way."

"Are you crazy?"

"She has energy for that?"

The road turns, becomes more narrow and gutted. There's a hushed whispering from trees. The darkness is thicker and dampness is in the air.

A forest? A ravine?

God no. I don't want to die now, not when so close....

But why not? Death would be fast and never again would an icy hand grab her heart. Never again would there be another crazed thought, another dream.

Never another dream? Of teaching? Dancing? Precious life?

A dream is a mirage. It is palm trees swaying in the breeze, water bubbling between stones while sand blows into your eyes and parched throat and the sun spears you onto the shifting mounds built of the same sand. A dream makes you put one weary foot in front of the other for something not real or real but elsewhere. Or real, even commonplace, but for others alone.

The road descends steeply. The wooden boots slide downhill. Her breath like a knife tears up and down her throat.

The road levels and her breath steadies slowly, painfully.

"Hans," says someone way back.

"*Hier,*" says the voice next to her.

She had forgotten him, his steps metal on stone. So this one marching with a bunch of women in total darkness is Hans.

The crunching comes closer.

"*Nicht Jetzt.*"

"*Warum?*"

"*Später*"

One pair of steps recedes, the other stomps alongside her

"What did they say?"

"One said, 'Not yet. Later.'"

"They're going to kill us."

"There's not enough of them."

"But they're armed."

"It's dark, you idiot."

"That's why he said, 'Later.'"

"Let's rush them."

"No, scatter."

"You're crazy."

It's just another dream. Another mirage.

"There's a truck full of them in the front!"

"They wouldn't dare kill us now. If the Americans come they'll just run."

"There's another truck in the back."

The dense dark trees whisper on the hills on both sides of the road. In the morning the forest will wake. Birds will dart between branches, squirrels will scamper up russet trunks, and deer with feet wide apart will lower their heads into brooks.

The forest hovers yards away. Her heart beats like a bird in its bone and sinew cage.

"Pass the word: The trucks are gone."

She hears the scream. Was it from her? And she hurls herself, or was she hurled, out and away, slamming into him, his rough military coat, belt buckle, and then his arm caught between them as they both fall, and she feels him under her, and others over her. "His throat," someone screams. "His gun!" "*Hilfe!*" he yells. Does she, or do they... before she rolls away? "Again," someone shrieks.

"Run!"

Shots. How many? Feet and legs speed around her on the ground. Then she is running and hits something hard and unrelenting. She falls over a body which feels like a loosely filled sack. She slides on something prickly and slippery, falling, rolling, then is up again flailing as she scrambles uphill. Panting ghosts surround her.

She halts. In the distance she hears scrambling, shooting. Around her is only her panting. Under her feet is steep, slippery ground. She leans to touch it covered with needles. She slumps onto it.

First, she smells the scent of pines. Then she feels the needles, dry, brittle, yet smooth, rolling under her fingers, her palms. She awakens and above her the straight russet trunks reach high with patches of the sky mashed into their dark crowns, the pearly light of dawn filtering through. It can't be. But above her trees sway, and under her palms needles roll.

She hears sound mashed like the sky against the crowns, mashed against the hushed whispers of the forest. Does it come from her mind? No, she can hear it.

No, God, it can't be.

The steep ground, the trees, spin, then stand still as the sound roars strong and jubilant. She dashes everywhere, slipping, rolling, falling, getting up, the forest surrounding her.

She must stop, listen. Hard as it is, she does. The sound clearly is downhill to her left. She scrambles towards it, finding a curving steep path which ends below a stone mass rising to the sky. On her knees, on her elbows; her feet slipping, her hands grabbing, she clambers up to the crescendo of the sound. She lies panting at the top of the cliff, her face against the craggy stone. She pulls herself to the edge and peeks over.

On the road below, a sea of cropped heads surround two khaki helmets. She presses her forehead on the stone. Her hands feel every crack. She raises her head and looks over again. Two khaki helmets are the hub of a whirling mass of cropped heads and striped dresses dashing everywhere. Figures hug, crash, separate, join, cry and yell.

A car like a box with its top cut off speeds towards them. A five-pointed white star on its hood, the strange car carrying four more khaki figures stops suddenly at the edge of the crowd. The crowd surrounds them. She yearns to fly down and join them, yell and scream, kiss and hug, be hugged and be kissed; touch those khaki men and run her fingers over their strange car.

Yet she lies, her heart pounding, her breath caught. And then, finally, hard and dry at first, emotion tears through her body before being dissolved by tears. It doesn't matter how long she sobs because blurred through her tears she can see them in the road. Only that matters.

Finally it is over. Slowly, trembling, she climbs down the crumbly steep slope to a brook which dashes clear over its stony bed, rushing between rocks, pebbles, boulders. She kneels at the edge of the water and dips her hands slowly into it. The ice-cold water eddies around her wrists. She cups her hands and brings them carefully to her lips. She drinks slowly savoring every drop. Then she dips her hands again, scooping more water, burying her face in its icy splendor. Leaning over the brook she splashes water on her face and neck, opens her dress to her waist. Something drops from her dress into the rushing water.

The brown, shapeless bread chunk falls into the silver-white cascade. She tries to grab it, but it's hurled against a rock, broken into small soggy bits. The creek sweeps them downstream as though wanting to purge itself. She laughs. The unaccustomed sound floats above the water, up the hill. She laughs again, then pulls her arms from her sleeves, lets her dress hang at her waist by the string belt. She splashes her uncovered breasts, feeling them smooth and cold, not like marble, she thinks, but flesh, trembling, alive. Reluctantly she pushes her arms into the sleeves and buttons the bodice.

She walks haltingly on the path from the brook, stopping to look often at the gray-white road between the green hills. The path is bathed in early morning sunshine as she leaves the tree-lined path. Ahead of her the road lies straight and empty until it curves gently. She can see them in the distance, the striped dresses, the khaki hats and the funny car. Jagged hills rise on both sides meeting the blue sky in jagged lines.

She would join them by simply lifting one foot, then the other, as she has done thousands of times. A ghostly dark and sharp leg jerks in front of her as she lifts her foot. On the gravel beginning at her feet lies her silent shadow, straight like a felled sentinel. Because the early morning sun is low behind her, her shadow is grotesque, long, skeletal and distorted.

She raises her arms and so does the shadow. She shakes her head and the shadow's head wobbles. She lifts her foot and the shadow exaggerates the long skeletal leg jerking. It does what she does, but in its own way. Whose shadow is it?

The sun puts a loving arm around her, and a breeze, light and fragrant caresses her cheeks. Under the grimy, striped dress, her body is fresh from the brook, her breasts are clean, cool, smooth, alive.

"All right," she instructs the shadow.

And they walk on the sunlit road together.

Shutters

Closed

"All right, I am not saying they should have resisted," says Mr. Goldman who usually takes out books on Jewish history. "No, I am not saying that. Although...." He waves a languid hand and raises his shoulders. "Anyway, there were other options like going into hiding or escaping if they were caught, just to mention two. But...." Another languid gesture follows, then Mr. Goldman says a pleasant good-bye and leaves the library.

Anna Petri sees him stop for a second just outside the door, his white hair lit up by the late-afternoon sun. She sits quietly at the reference desk, looking at the door well after Mr. Goldman leaves. Then she tidies the desk.

She walks out the same door into the same late mellow sunshine and walks home slowly along the seven steep blocks to the small apartment where she has been living since her husband died three years before.

It is Friday afternoon. She will eat, change and go to services. She decided yesterday she would. She has not gone to Temple for at least four, maybe five, months.

But, once home, she sits at the window overlooking roofs, chimneys, trees and in the distance a shimmering stretch of the Pacific Ocean. She sits until the sky fades, then darkens, and the lights go on in the streets, in houses, and a low-flying plane makes its twinkling way across the sky.

When she was younger, Anna Petri would argue with the many Mr. Goldmans. She would explain, or try to explain realities—circumstances, events, conditions, even though she soon realized it was futile. Realities were resisted with skill and determination. Yet she wouldn't give up, would try again and again. Yet there she sat today, proper reference librarian, proper employee of the public library, silent. Well, one should never argue with a patron.

Was that it? Or was it that she was older, maybe wiser? Or was it that she had not heard comments like these for some time? A new generation has grown up. There are questions these days instead of reproaches.

Whatever the case, there she sat and had not responded to what Mr. Goldman had said. He had appeared at her desk with a question concerning the catalogue, had spotted a book on the Holocaust somebody had left on the desk, forgot about the catalogue, and charged into a discourse.

Well, Mr. Goldman didn't know to whom he was talking. But then, others did know, and would still make similar comments. Not lately, though. Mr. Goldman was behind the times.

Anna Petri doesn't go to Temple Saturday either. She takes a long walk trying to think of anything other than Mr. Goldman. She walks in the park under towering eucalyptus trees, enveloped in their scent. She walks along the beach on the hard-packed, wet sand, then she eats lunch in a small cafe at a table upon which someone has sketched a little figure, its abstract arms spread wide.

She can't think of anything else.

Neither can she think of anything else that night sitting in her bed or sitting at the window— nor can she the next day—a quiet, melancholy Sunday, spent again walking.

But why? Well, she is older. Instead of anger, there is pain. That is some sort of an answer, but not the answer she needs. Slowly, gradually, a desire to go home surfaces. Now that is totally illogical. There is no home. That house, not seen for years, inhabited by strangers is certainly not "home." Also, it is thousands of miles away, in another country, on another continent.

And hadn't she decided never, ever, to return to that house?

This town square could be anywhere here in Hungary, Anna Berger thinks. It's deserted in the summer noon heat, except for a woman with a small girl in a red play-suit sitting on a bench, a tree drooping like a half-closed umbrella above them. They eat ice cream cones, slowly, dreamily.

Anna Petri, held tight by the rented car's seatbelt, stares at the square. The benches seem new, can't possibly be the same. Maybe even the trees have been planted since then. The houses, though, are the same. But at the far end of the square is a sidewalk cafe with small tables and bright yellow and orange chairs. There was no cafe before.

She stares into her compact mirror, then tosses it back into her handbag. Finally, she unbuckles the seat belt and opens the door. The sun shoots tiny burning arrows into her eyes. For a second she holds onto the car, then tucks the handbag firmly under her arm and crosses the square, passing the woman and girl. A young blonde man looks up, then throws what was left of an apple to the fluttering pigeons.

Around the corner, the street lies quiet in the sunshine. It is familiar, but just in the vague, distant way it seemed familiar in many dreams: hard, white light, and the short-ened noontime shadows of the acacia trees—huge uneven blotches on the sidewalk and the street cobblestones. She used to skip from one to another, in and out of shadows. Do kids here still do that?

The houses are smaller than she remembers, yet just as solid, facing each other just as sedately. A girl in a red cotton dress passes her. Is she fourteen, like Anna had been when they shoved her family into boxcars half a century ago? Then a man passes, fortyish, carrying a tennis racket.

They could be from anywhere—the man, the girl. They are not particular to this town, this street, not part of her dreams, or of her nightmares. *Good,* thinks Anna Petri. She will go to the house, since she is here, had decided to come, *did* come. She will make it short.

She comes upon the house as she had planned, from the other side of the street. The house is smaller than she remembers but otherwise it is the same with its buff brick walls, solid brown gate arched at the top, red tile roof. She stops across the street, leans against a tree, her palms flat against the dry, crumbling bark, and stands for a while. Finally she detaches herself from the tree and walks out of its shadow, into the glare of the road, then over to the other side.

The gate latch is hot, like it used to get in the violent summer sun. She presses it down and pushes the heavy door open. Inside, the passage is cool, as it used to be, and dark after the outside glare. And it would surely echo, although she would not sing now walking through it, as she used to, never tiring of playing with that echo. Now only her steps echo, her heels hard on the smooth stone.

At the open end of the passage had been the garden with the evergreens that were so hard to keep alive in this climate and soil, but were lovely dark green against the flaming tulips in the spring and the roses in the summer.

The evergreens are gone.

New, different flowers, shrubs are nicely laid out. The pump is the same. Not much you can do about pumps, can you?

And they hadn't done anything about the house either: the L shaped building, like an arm around the garden; the long, open porch with windows and doors opening onto it; and the first door to the left. They are all as she has many times dreamed. She would dash toward the door, in her dreams, through the echoing passage—dash toward it, throw it open, and the little bell would cling.

The door is locked.

She walks along the porch to the family entrance.

That door is wide open.

Inside, in the small tile vestibule is a clothes rack with a child's baseball cap dangling from one of the hooks and a pair of small sneakers, one lying on its side, on the shiny tile floor, the very same tile floor of many colors. Once she had counted just how many colors but has forgotten since. She wishes she could get down on her knees, count the colors.

A woman emerges from the dining room, in her twenties, pretty, a bit plump, in a print cotton dress, her light brown hair brushing her shoulders.

"Good day," says Anna Petri.

"Good day."

What now before this threshold?

"My name is Anna Petri."

"Yes...."

"I was wondering—you see, we used to live in this house.... I mean, we owned it. Actually, my grandfather built it. And—and I was born here, and our name was Remenyi, and my father...."

"Oh, yes, I was told about your family."

The woman murmurs her name. Anna Petri doesn't get it. She says they moved here three years ago, from another town, she and her family. Bought the house then. Love it.

Anna Petri stands at the threshold, looking at the floor of many colors and thinks she never noticed the red and black tiles make such sinuous curves between the blues and greens. It is amazing she had not noticed, but then she might never have looked at the tiles from where she is standing or might never have looked at them in this particular way.

"Would you like to come in?"

"Thank you," says Anna Petri. "I actually came to—I mean, I wonder whether I may...."

"But of course you may see the house."

Gratefully, Anna Petri smiles and steps over the threshold.

They walk into the dining room. The room looks like a dream in which images keep sliding over each other that just don't belong together: the high windows, the high doors, the high ceiling imposing upon the sparse modern furniture, the pretty modern chandelier. The woman.

The woman is saying something about opening, or unlocking, doors, something about the house being divided into two apartments. But she has keys, the woman.

And, "Why don't you just go around and look at the house on your own."

She is kind and Anna Petri should have thanked her, but all she can manage is a nod.

The woman stands watching Anna Petri walk into the living room and from there to the corridor in the center of the house. She hears the click of locks and then the hitting of wood against wood as the pocket doors are slid open to their wide frames.

She wanders. The house—in spite of the space and light and air—feels tight, dark, even suffocating. This passes only after she sits on the window sill in what used to be her room.

She sits sideways on the wide sill, her back against the frame, her feet pulled up, as she used to as a girl. To her right, outside the open window, is the garden. The walnut tree and the table under it used to be there. On summer nights they would sit around the table, and the crickets would chirp, but now there is no tree, no table. Pretty pink flowers grow instead. Anna Petri wonders what they are called.

Her bed used to be near the window. On the night-stand was the lamp with the shade that threw colors and shapes on the ceiling while her mother sat on her bed and told funny stories, and then her father would come in, and they would talk. She wishes she could recall about what, but she recalls only how it felt to be tucked in warm, with her parents there, talking quietly until she drifted into sleep.

But that was long ago, long before what happened later.

Was she really that child once? When she finally stands and walks from the room into the corridor, she realizes she has no idea what kind of furniture now is in her room after having sat in the window for at least half an hour.

Her father's medical office is furnished as a living room, beige and brown. It used to be white, white walls, desks, everything except for the instruments glittering on glass shelves behind glass doors, glittering like silver on summer mornings with sunlight hitting them. And she would dash in bare footed and in her nightgown before the patients entered, hug her father in his white starched smock.

There were no questions then, just that white-clad magician in his white and silver world. Magician? But couldn't magicians.... Only in fairy tales could benevolent magicians ward off evil hordes. But there were those fairy tale mornings with their quick hugs in this room, with the talking heard through the waiting room door, with the summer morning sounds coming through the window—the cluck-cluck of the pump, a distant laugh, the quick patter of slippers along the porch. How much had died gradually during the five years before that horrible summer morning?

It was June 10, 1944.

"Dr. Remenyi," one of the gendarmes had said in this room. The other gendarme just stood by looking at the floor in front of his boots. Their bayonets glittered in the sun streaming through the window. Her father stood behind his desk. Her mother stood next to him.

Where was she? Now, the gendarmes stood in the very center of the room. So here they were in this room—not in this room, but in that silver-and-white office—the three of them close. Wherever she was standing, it was close to them, she is sure. The three of them faced those two with their bayonets.

Outside the window was the garden, the soil rich, deep brown, the shrubs hard, dark, shiny green, and the roses in full bloom, pink, white, yellow, red.

No one was in the garden.

No one was in the rest of the house, in the ransacked locked rooms with the blood-red seals drying into shiny, blood-red blisters on the white doors.

No one was in the street either in the glare of the sun on the sidewalk while the gendarme, the silent one, affixed a seal to the gate.

Then they walked, their steps sounding like glass being crushed in an empty, abandoned room.

———

In her parents' bedroom Anna Petri leans against the brown tile stove, high and intact which stands like a medieval tower in the midst of a modern city grown around it. The smooth glazed tiles cool her back and palms. Something happened the day before the gendarmes came, forty-one years ago, almost to this very day. She was born in this room fifty-five years ago and she almost died in this room forty-one years ago. Just what happened?

"It didn't work," said her father that morning. He stood at the window, with his back to the street.

There was no need to ask what didn't work. It was the fourth escape attempt. There had been late night talks with strangers, meetings with trusted friends, secrecy, excitement. New names were learned, family stories and situations invented, memorized in haste, forgotten for new stories memorized in even greater haste.

"It's too risky for them," said her mother sitting on the edge of the bed, her hands clasping the edge of the mattress.

———

One of her parents said since she was almost fifteen she could understand, that what would come could be so terrible. There was no way of knowing. What matters was somehow the three of them came to an understanding. Her mother had awakened her at dawn and asked her to come to their bedroom. What decision had they expected from her, one asked without words?

If she had agreed.... The three of them standing in this room, her father's deft doctor's hands, holding the shining steel and glass syringe....

Surely, for them it would have been better. And for her? After all, nothing had been said. They just questioned each other without words far from each other across the room. At what point did they meet somewhere between where they had been, she at the stove, her father at the window, her mother sitting on the bed? Meeting and yet not touching. But it felt much more than touching, the standing so close.

Anna Petri lets go of the stove as she had that morning. She steps this way and that. Maybe they were standing here. Close. Silent. Finally, there was just her father's nod and his wan smile. They hugged and held each other tight.

It is to them she has come, not to this shell of a house. Anna Petri stands still in the center of the room.

She doesn't notice the woman entering, but she is standing at the waiting room door or what used to be the waiting room door.

"This was my father's office," she tells the woman.

They both stand quietly. She doesn't know how long.

"You know, they still talk about your father," the woman says, "some older people who knew him. They say he was the best doctor they ever had. And a fine man, too. He cared, they say."

Silence again.

"They told me how upset they were."

"They did?"

"Why, yes. They never thought he would ever want to leave town."

"*Want* to leave town?"

"They didn't even know where he went. A woman told me he had moved to some other town, she wasn't sure where. Then an old man across the street—he passed away about a year ago—said the doctor and his family had left for America."

"We did not leave for America. We were rounded up. We were apprehended in this very room. In June 1944. They were standing right here, my mother and my father, right here, where this sofa is now. The gendarmes were standing...." She looks around, steps to the right, then to the left, with fast short steps. "I think where this table is. I can't remember. Their bayonets were sparkling, so it must have been near the window, and it was in the morning and the sun was shining; and here was my father's desk, and on the wall, his diploma, and it was in Latin, except for his surname. I guess there was no way to translate that, so there was his name—'Remenyi'—and just why would they say we moved or that we went to America? They know we didn't. We left in the bright sunlight, the street was deserted, the shutters were closed in all the houses along this street, and the next, and the next, and the next; and I have nightmares about those shutters. And now they say...."

Her voice breaks abruptly in the air that has become sparse.

The young woman leans against the door frame, staring with sad and serious eyes.

"I see," she says.

"But just why would they say...?" Anna Petri sputters again, to this woman in her pretty floral print dress, this young woman living in her house. She asks as though she could know. "Just why would they say...?"

The woman crosses the beige-and-brown room and lays her hand on Anna Petri's arm.

"They still talk about your father."

"But why would they say...?"

"I don't know. Maybe it's because they lived here— when— I don't know. I'm just glad I didn't have to—I mean, I'm glad I didn't live here. What I mean is, I'm glad I didn't live then."

Anna Petri walks slowly under the acacia trees, their shadows long now, almost touching, between the solid houses facing each other across the street.

Some shutters are open, some are closed, and some are open just a crack.

Afterword

In this book of twelve short stories, Frances Fabri (nee Sarika Frances Ladanyi) describes what she experienced in extreme and macabre situations. Her taped oral history at the Holocaust Center of Northern California confirms these stories happened to her and the people she knew. She made an interesting creative decision to present her stories through the eyes of various participants, including victims, bystanders and perpetrators.

Frances Fabri was a fourteen year old girl when her secure way of life in a Hungarian town abruptly ended. Her father was a well established physician, and she described the atmosphere of her home as cheerful and warm. Three months after the Germans invaded Hungary in 1944, she and her parents were deported to Auschwitz. She never saw her father again. Miraculously, she and her mother survived in four additional camps and were able to support one another. At Altenberg, a labor camp, she was the youngest of 400 slave laborers at the age of 15. While on a death march from the German munitions plant where they worked, she and her mother were liberated by American soldiers in 1945.

Frances had extraordinary perceptiveness as a teenager, with a keen eye for the character and behavior of the people in this world of horror. It was her nature to look for acts of kindness, and ways in which people helped each other. The short stories she wrote during her mature years tell of these memories in the midst of violence.

Emigrating to the United States in 1956, Frances received a Masters Degree in history from Hofstra College in New York. When she moved to San Francisco in the 1970's she recognized the need for awareness and remembrance of the Holocaust. She developed a program for interviewing survivors at the Holocaust Center of Northern California, of which she was a founder. She trained volunteers in the early 1980's and together they created an archive of witness testimony. In the 1990's Frances was a founding member of *Tikvah Acharey Hashoah*, an organization for survivor self-help and advocacy for social services.

For over thirty years, Frances continued to write and revise her stories. Each one is an astonishing gem, demonstrating transcendent courage and compassion. They are published posthumously in her honor, and in hope of creating deeper understanding.

—Eva W. Maiden